The Tale  ash

Dinosaur Adventure

To LUKE

HAPPY READING !!

M.C

The Tales of Fluke & Tash

Dinosaur Adventure

MARK ELVY

Available from

www.ypdbooks.com
and
www.flukeandtash.com

A CIP catalogue record for this book is available from the British Library.

ISBN 978-1-9998910-0-8

Book layout by Clare Brayshaw

Prepared and printed by:

York Publishing Services Ltd
64 Hallfield Road
Layerthorpe
York YO31 7ZQ

Tel: 01904 431213

Website: www.yps-publishing.co.uk

Glossary of Dinosaur names
Phonetic spelling...

Alamosaurus	(Ah-la-mow-sore-us)
Anatotitan	(An-at-oh-tie-tan)
Ankylosaurus	(An-kie-loh-sore-us)
Bugenasaura	(Boo-jen-ah-sore-ah)
Diceratops	(Die-ker-ah-tops)
Gorgosaurus	(Gor-goh-sore-us)
Lophorhothons	(Lof-oh-roh-thon)
Mosasaurus	(Moe-za-sore-us)
Nanotyrannus	(Nan-oh-tie-ran-us)
Pachycephalosaurus	(Pack-i-kef-al-oh-sore-russ)
Panoplosaurus	(Pan-op-loh-sore-us)
Pteranodons	(Tear-ann-owe-dons)
Stygimolochs	(Stij-i-mol-ok)

Triceratops	(Tri-serra-tops)
Troodon	(Troh-oh-don)
Tyrannosaurus	(Tie-ran-oh-sore-us)
Velociraptor	(Vel-oss-ee-rap-tor)

65 million years BC –
Colorado, North America,

Tuesday, about lunchtime...

The young Alamosaurus heaved his considerable bulk up the side of the hill. Reaching the crest, he padded as far to the edge as his parents would let him go. He'd had strict instructions not to get too close, as it was dangerous. His mum would remind him, *'Amos dear, remember not to get too close to the edge, you know how clumsy you are and it's a long way down!'*

Amos made his way to his normal spot, which gave him uninterrupted views across the valley. He stood and stared into the midday sky, the bright sunshine caused him to squint and he watched in envy at the graceful scene that unfolded before his eyes.

'Pteranodons don't realise just how lucky they are, flying around like that,' he muttered to himself, wishing that one day he could fly instead of walking everywhere. The giant flying reptiles were performing some breath-taking acrobatics, using the air currents to circle high above the ground. Occasionally swooping down to skim the surface of the large lake looking for a fish dinner, no doubt. *Fish dinner? Yuk!* Thought Amos, a herbivore, which meant he was a plant-eater and couldn't stomach the thought of eating any meat or fish.

Next he spied a Pachycephalosaurus in such a hurry, charging through bushes and ferns, either playing a game of chase or being chased, you just never knew. Amos then heard the sound that caused most dinosaurs to shiver with fear. The unmistakable roar of the dreaded T-Rex echoing off the canyon walls. That answered his question, the young Pachycephalosaurus was running away from danger, because when a bad tempered and hungry T-Rex was nearby the whole area went into hiding.

Amos was glad he was up high and away from danger. His thoughts drifted to his best friend Nat. He was an Anatotitan, and had been missing for several days now. His concerned parents had been frantically trying to locate him and had spread the word as far as they could, but nobody had seen him around and you couldn't really miss him, as he was nearly nine metres long. Amos shuddered and just hoped and prayed that Nat was safe and well, and that the hungry T-Rex wasn't involved in Nat's disappearance.

Amos continued his gazing and spied *the volcano,* far, far away on the horizon. Plumes of smoke drifted lazily from the top, forming a hazy cloud that just seemed to hang in the air waiting for any breeze to blow it away. Rumours were rife that *the volcano* was home to unknown creatures, who lived deep inside near the centre of the earth and only came out to capture lost dinosaurs that dared to venture too close.

His parents and all the dinosaur elders had said that if you got too close you were never seen again. The thought of being captured and not seeing his friends or parents sent shivers down his spine. He noticed that even the flying Pteranodons kept well away from the rim of the volcano – circling around using the air currents, they would turn at the last minute when they felt they got too close.

He did wonder whether it was just a tale spun by the dinosaur elders to stop the youngsters from wandering off on their own, but he wasn't really worried as *the volcano* was a good few days walk away and walking wasn't one of his favourite pastimes.

Just as he was about to turn round and head back home, something caught his attention. A new creature with four small figures on its back had suddenly appeared out of nowhere and joined in flying with the Pteranodons.

Frowning, Amos wondered where this new creature had come from and decided to stay a bit longer and watch, as the strangers flew around, weaving here there and everywhere. He could hear what sounded like laughter and sounds of whooping coming from the sky.

The newcomer was approached by two stray Pteranodons that had joined the display. Larger, and a slightly different colour to the rest, they had previously been keeping their distance, when they suddenly swooped in fast and appeared to attack the stranger, causing it to spin wildly out of control and to tumble from the sky.

Amos watched in horror as the large Pteranodons plucked two of the smaller creatures from the sky and rapidly flew away, heading towards the smouldering volcano. The other two figures managed to stay aboard but plummeted towards the lake directly below. A loud splash followed, and then silence.

Amos wondered what to do next, then decided to go and investigate. There was nothing he could do for the creatures that had been captured by the Pteranodons, but he could try and help the others that might be in trouble, as the lake was deep. He turned around and headed as fast as he could down the steep hill, hoping he could get there in time, curious to know who the strangers were.

Present day...

Hunting for dinosaurs

S he was secretly watching and stalking the dinosaur from the long grass and had carefully concealed herself as any good hunter would have done. Poised and ready to strike, she prepared herself. There was no way for the creature to escape, it was boxed in, escape was impossible.

A split second before she was about to pounce and leap on her prey, a voice rang out, 'Fluke, Tash, dinner's ready,' and she watched in dismay as Fluke tore down the garden and stepped on the plastic toy dinosaur that Tash had been ready to pounce on.

'Fluke, look what you've done!' exclaimed Tash, as she walked over to the small toy that was now in two pieces, as the head had fallen off after Fluke had trodden on it in his haste to get some dinner. Shaking her head she picked up the broken toy dinosaur and wondered what the neighbours would say. Tash had crept into next door's garden when they were out and *'borrowed'* one of their plastic dinosaur toys.

Hoping the kids wouldn't notice the damage, she crept under the fence and replaced the broken toy, having tried to repair it first as best she could, and padded off, quietly whistling to herself, hoping nobody had seen her.

She joined Fluke in the kitchen and started to eat her dinner. Once finished, she wiped the back of her paw and cleaned her whiskers, and muttered 'all that hunting makes you hungry Fluke.' Gazing at Fluke's empty bowl she sniggered 'So what's your excuse, why are you so hungry? I've noticed you haven't joined me in the great dinosaur hunt.'

'Hunting's easy Tash,' grinned Fluke, 'I've been the busy one, excavating old dinosaur bones!'

'You mean you've been helping dad dig holes in the garden. He's planting seeds and you've been digging them up again,' she laughed and glanced down at Fluke's mucky paws, and laughed even louder when she followed a trail of dirty paw prints starting at the patio door and leading up to Fluke's dog bowl. 'Mum's going to go mad Fluke, look at the mess you've made, and you can't deny it, the paw prints lead right up to your bowl!' and with that she went back outside in the sunshine and flopped onto a garden chair, having first plumped up the soft cushion.

Fluke looked down at the paw prints and knew he'd be in trouble yet again. He chuckled to himself as he swapped the food bowls around, making it look like Tash had the dirty paws not him, and sniggering, he crept outside and joined Tash on the patio.

'So Tash...' he whispered carefully looking around, checking to see that mum and dad weren't listening, 'it must be time to get the magic case out again and go on another adventure.'

'Yes Fluke, tonight, normal time, we'll be off on a new adventure and I'm really looking forward to it. So tell me, you're not even a tiny bit nervous about going back in time to visit the dinosaurs then?' said Tash, knowing how dangerous but exciting their new time travelling adventure could be.

'Yeah, a little bit nervous Tash. I mean huge dinosaurs everywhere with big sharp teeth, who wouldn't be scared, but I have a plan to stay safe,' he confirmed.

'Plan? What plan is that then?'

'I just have to make sure that I can run faster than you Tash,' he laughed.

'Yeah thanks Fluke, let's just hope it doesn't come down to a race between you, me and a Tyrannosaurus, as I don't fancy your chances!' Tash giggled. 'C'mon, let's pop over to the Nummers tree stump and see if they're at home, and get some advice before we go. We know they've been around for thousands of years, but maybe even the Nummers aren't that old.'

They headed over to visit their small secret friends and waited patiently as Tash knocked on their little wooden door carefully concealed in the base of the tree stump.

Prehistoric Nummers...

The little door opened and out strode Papa Nummer, who greeted his two friends and then gazed at Fluke's mucky paws. 'So Fluke, how many dinosaur bones have you managed to dig up?' he asked casually and caught Tash chuckling to herself.

Fluke looked all round and then over his shoulder to see who may be listening. Glancing back to his friends, confident nobody was eavesdropping into their conversation, he whispered, 'So do you want to see them then?', and promptly disappeared behind a bush for a few seconds. He could be heard rummaging around and seconds later he returned with a bag slung over his shoulder.

Tash looked over to Papa Nummer and grinned, both watching with amusement at the antics of Fluke. Letting the bag drop to the floor, he busied himself and attempted to untie the secure knot.

'Why is it....,' he mumbled to himself, 'that when you tie up a bag with a loose knot, and then you come to undo the bag, the knot has mysteriously got *sooooo* much tighter!' His large paws struggled until he triumphantly shouted out 'Ta-da!', delved deep inside and laid out his selection of dinosaur bones onto the grass.

'Mmmm...' said Tash closely inspecting the items laid out before them, 'I didn't realise you were a *Palaeontologist* Fluke, I must say it's a fine collection,' she was nodding her pretend approval and then slyly winked to Papa Nummer when Fluke had his back turned.

'Neither did I...,' shrugged Fluke looking confused and scratching his ear, '... just checking though Tash, but what exactly is a *paleo...*, *palao... palatolo...* you know that thingamajig type person that you just called me?'

'A palaeontologist is a scientist that studies fossils, Fluke,' she confirmed to a slightly bewildered looking Fluke.

'Scientist?' he puffed his chest out in pride, 'I've been called a few things but never a scientist!' and began to put his collection of bones back in the bag, tied a new knot and dragged the contents back to his hideaway behind the bush.

'You do realise...' whispered Papa Nummer watching Fluke disappear for a few seconds, 'that those bones were a pork chop bone, leg of lamb bone and a recent T-bone steak?'

Tash sniggered, 'Yes I know what they were – I saw Fluke rummaging in the dustbin early this morning, they're leftovers from the BBQ mum and dad had at the weekend, but don't let on that we know!'

'So, back to business,' Fluke said as he strolled back and re-joined Papa Nummer and Tash. 'We're off again tonight Papa, a long way, and I mean a *very* long way back in time, to go and see some dinosaurs. Any advice that you can give us?'

'Be extra careful and run fast if you're being chased!' Papa Nummer joked and then turned round and whispered to his wife who was stood in their doorway.

Tash heard snippets of the whispered discussion taking place, 'You can ask them,' he confirmed and smiled as Mama Nummer stepped outside.

'Every time you go on these wonderful adventures we sit here in our little tree stump home and wonder what it would be like to travel like you two. It must be great fun,' Mama Nummer said rather bashfully, 'and we were talking the other night, and just wondering if it would be possible, but only if you're OK with it, if you could see you're way to letting us, but only if there's enough room mind you, but we're only small, and we promise not to get in your way....' Mama Nummer continued nervously, whilst Fluke looked at Tash with a confused look. 'can we come with you...?' finished Papa Nummer, looking at his wife, 'we'll be here all night long waiting for you to ask them my dear!'

'You want to come with us on our new adventure?' confirmed Fluke, a huge grin spread across his face. Turning to Tash he asked, 'What do you reckon partner, do we have the room on our case?'

Laughing, Tash said 'We'll make room Fluke! Of course you can come along, it'll be great having you both with us, and you can help me keep Fluke out of mischief!'

The group of four huddled together, plans were made and it was agreed they would meet in the spare room later that evening.

'See you two about midnight,' said Fluke merrily, and followed Tash who was headed back to the patio to finish the hard job she'd started earlier of an afternoon catnap.

Fashion show...

It was always the same. Whenever Fluke and Tash planned a new time travelling trip the minutes seemed to drag whilst they were waiting for mum and dad to go to bed before they could start their new adventure. Today was no different. The afternoon wore on, until eventually late evening arrived and mum thankfully started to yawn and headed upstairs, closely followed by dad.

'Thirty minutes?' whispered Fluke looking at the cuckoo clock, as they always liked a friendly bet as to how long it took dad to start snoring.

'Bet you it's only twenty five minutes this time Fluke,' she laughed.

In reality only twenty minutes passed before the bedroom lights were extinguished and the familiar snoring could be heard from the bedroom.

'Right c'mon Fluke, let's get the magic case out of the wardrobe, set the co-ordinates and wait for the Nummers to turn up,' said Tash. She headed quietly up the steep stairs and was passed halfway up by an eager Fluke, who fairly bounded up the stairs taking two steps at a time.

'Out the way slow coach...' he whispered passing Tash, 'told you I was faster than you. I'll have no worries about the race between you, me and Mr T-Rex!'

Entering the spare room they noticed two small heads peeking out from under the bed. Surprised to find the Nummers waiting for them Tash asked, 'how long have you been waiting?'

'We didn't hear or see you come in the house,' Fluke said wondering how they had got past him whilst he had been laying on the living room floor.

'We've found lots of ways to get indoors without being spotted,' Papa Nummer said grinning from ear-to-ear, 'it's our speciality, getting into places without anybody finding out.'

'Some guard dog you are!' said Tash turning to Fluke, who shrugged and headed over to the wardrobe.

Mama Nummer spoke up, 'is there anything we can do to help?' watching Fluke open the doors, move clothes along the rail and rummage deep inside. Dragging out their ancient looking magic case he left it on the floor beside Tash and quietly closed the wardrobe doors.

'Are you sure it's safe?' said a hesitant Papa Nummer, casting a nervous glance at the beat up old case completely covered in scratches and dents. 'I mean it looks really old, are you sure it won't fall to pieces?'

Shaking her head and ignoring Papa Nummer's comments, Tash fiddled with the co-ordinates. '65 Million years BC is the date I think we agreed on,' she stepped back and undid the case locks, which caused the lid to spring open. 'Time to see what costumes the case has chosen for us…' she muttered and proceeded to rummage inside.

Retrieving her costume she proceeded to get changed and watched as Fluke and the Nummers delved inside. The scene, thought Tash, reminded her of a changing room at a fashion show – discarded costumes strewn over the floor until they were all happily wearing their new outfits.

'Well, don't we look cool…' exclaimed Fluke looking Tash and the Nummers up and down, 'Long beige safari shorts, thick beige cotton shirts and safari hiking boots – just call me Indiana Jones!' he joked.

'More like Mr. Jones the local bird spotter from down the road,' Tash giggled and proceeded to complete her outfit with a beige satchel, which contained several items such as a set of maps, a compass, a battery powered torch, a pair of binoculars and a length of rope. Once the satchel was slung over her shoulder she busied herself checking the co-ordinates on the magic case.

First class or economy seats...?

Satisfied the co-ordinates were set, Tash leapt aboard and waited patiently for Fluke to take his normal place behind her. The Nummers were hesitating and stood nervously watching.

'Welcome to Fluke and Tash airways...' joked Fluke, 'where excitement and adventure are always guaranteed! If you could please make your way to your allocated seats as departure time is 12:22 and we can't have you being late for your first flight with us,' he continued pretending to check the Nummers' tickets. 'First class or economy class seats, madam?' he asked a bemused Mama Nummer, who was now beginning to relax and enjoy herself.

'Oh, without a doubt first class please,' she smiled.

'OK, up front behind the pilot, who for today's flight is captain Tash,' Fluke continued the joke, 'and you sir must have the economy seat,' he said to Papa Nummer, 'if you could squeeze in behind Mama Nummer and please leave enough room for me!'

The Nummers were wedged in between Tash and Fluke, who eventually took his position at the rear of the case. Watching Tash turn the case handle three times he glanced at the red neon light cast by the digital clock and noticed with satisfaction the time was exactly 12:22. 'On time as usual Captain!' and his ears started to flap as the case began the now familiar spinning, the wind picked up, and they promptly vanished from the spare room.

Whoa they're big birds...

The magic case and its four passengers materialised into a bright midday sun, and very nearly ploughed headlong into a flock of flying reptiles. Tash was at the front steering and weaving a course through the circling Pteranodons who continued their graceful flight and allowed the four newcomers to join in with their high altitude antics.

'Welcome to Colorado, North America!' grinned Tash, turning around to see the faces of the Nummers. A mixture of fear and excitement was the first impression their small faces showed. Mama Nummer was holding onto Tash's shirt firmly but began to relax and enjoy herself. Fluke meanwhile, sat at the rear, was whooping with joy as the case banked sharply and started to follow two of the large birds.

'Will you take a look at the stunning scenery...' he hollered, 'and whoa they're big birds!' he shouted and ducked as one of the Pteranodons swooped overhead causing a brief shadow to fall across them, partially blocking out the sunlight. 'Look everyone, down below; herds of dinosaurs roaming across the land! It's just like the film *Jurassic Park* or watching that television series *Walking with Dinosaurs.*'

'Let's just hope our story doesn't have a similar ending to the film then Fluke, as I don't want to get trapped or chased by Velociraptors and a T-Rex!' shivered Tash nervously.

The four passengers aboard *Fluke and Tash Airways* continued to weave in and around the Pteranodons. 'Those two look different from the rest,' Tash shouted above the wind, pointing to two of the larger flying reptiles. She noted the long bony crest on top of their heads, a type of rudder maybe, which probably helped their steering and assisted with their superb flying capabilities.

'Different colour as well. Notice they have a red-crested head *and* they keep swooping closer than the rest! Steer clear from them will you Tash, I've got a bad feeling about those two,' commented Fluke, suddenly feeling nervous.

'Hang on tight everybody, I think we're being attacked!' exclaimed Tash seconds later, as the two reptiles joined forces and charged at an amazing speed, parting at the last second before impact. One reptile went left and the other swooped right under the case, their huge wingspans and large leathery wings causing some severe air turbulence.

The one that flew underneath used its large bony crest to knock the underside of the case on purpose. Tash lost steering, and the case began to spin wildly out of control.

I've really got to take swimming lessons...

The case began a rapid free-fall, spinning and turning wildly out of control. Fluke was getting dizzy and it took all his best efforts just to hang on and stay aboard. He groaned and watched as the two large reptiles turned sharply and swooped overhead in formation, side-by-side, easily plucking Papa Nummer and Mama Nummer free from the case.

'Noooooo!' Fluke shouted in dismay as he saw his two friends, the Nummers, being firmly held by sharp talons, dangling underneath the two rapidly disappearing Pteranodons. The reptiles disappeared from sight, as the magic case caused an almighty splash and landed firmly in the middle of a very large lake, which thankfully was directly below them, partially cushioning their landing.

The case disappeared briefly under the water and then bobbed back to the surface. Tash was hanging onto the front and Fluke was partially submerged in the crystal clear water, but still holding on to the case's handle.

'I've really got to learn how to swim…' muttered Fluke as he clambered back on-board and sat shivering in soaking wet clothes, '*and* I feel sea sick!' he complained, as the case bobbed up and down on the small waves it had caused when it crashed into the lake.

'What's happened to the Nummers?' asked a stunned Tash, who glanced nervously towards the distant shore line, noting the edge of the lake was some way off.

'They've gone Tash!'

'Gone? What do you mean gone?'

'Taken, kidnapped or whatever you want to call it. They were plucked from right in front of me by those two large reptiles, and I couldn't do a thing to help them,' said Fluke, clearly upset.

Shaking her head in shock, Tash tried to take control of the situation. 'We'll find them Fluke and get them back safe and sound, but first we have to get to the shoreline and out of the water, so start paddling!'

'Paddling? What with Tash? We don't have any oars, and in case you hadn't noticed we're sat on a magic suitcase *not* in a boat,' Fluke waited to see how Tash proposed to get them out of this predicament.

'Paws Fluke, we have to use our paws,' confirmed Tash who dipped her paw into the water and started a paddling motion, which to

Fluke's surprise actually began to move their case.

'So this is what they call doggy paddling then Tash,' joked Fluke, eagerly dipping his paw into the water to help Tash, desperate to get back to dry land.

'Whoa, easy with the water...!' exclaimed Tash, who was getting drenched by an over eager Fluke, whose frantic paddling was causing them to get thoroughly soaked, 'and we seem to be going round in circles Fluke, so try dipping your paw into the water the other side of the case.'

It was true, they were just spinning around in circles and not getting any closer to the shoreline. Changing tactics, they began to paddle slowly, carefully straightening themselves, and both noticed the edge of the lake getting closer.

Kneeling on the case and gazing down into the clear water below, Fluke noticed his reflection staring back at him, and then he thought he noticed a dark shape that seemed to swim past. Something brushed past his submerged paw causing him to shout out in alarm. 'What was that...?' he said nervously lifting his paw from the water and continued to gaze into the watery depths. 'I don't think we're alone Tash. Something else is in the lake with us, and whatever it is, it's huge and touched my paw as it swam past!'

'Keep paddling Fluke, we can't sit out here all day, and if there is something in the lake we don't want to be sat here at night time all alone in the dark!'

The thought of sitting in the middle of a dinosaur infested lake at night, in the dark, all alone, caused Fluke to paddle furiously, when he heard Tash start humming *'Duuun dun, duuun dun, dun dun dun dun dun dun dun dun'* the scary theme tune to the *Jaws* film they had watched several times.

'Oh you're *soooo* not funny Tash!' Fluke muttered, but annoyed he hadn't thought of humming it first to try and scare Tash!

'Count your toes Fluke, better make sure Mr Jaws hasn't got peckish and nibbled them off!' Tash laughed, and then suddenly stopped mid-chuckle as she also felt something swim past. She too withdrew her paw and stared into the water, when whatever it was got closer to the surface. The creature partially broke the surface but before Tash could get a good look it promptly disappeared again. 'You weren't joking Fluke, I've just seen something swim past, and it looks huge!'

'Nessie,' muttered Fluke.

'Don't call me a *Jessie* just because I don't want my toes nibbled off!' said Tash defensively.

'I said *Nessie*, as in the Loch Ness monster. I know we're not in Scotland, but it could be a Nessie type of dinosaur here in Colorado.'

Full reverse...

They both sat astride the case for a few minutes, waiting patiently. The case bobbed up and down on the slight swell the large creature had caused, neither wanted to be the first to start paddling.

'You first Tash, you're the leader,' said Fluke.

'It was probably a large salmon or trout, or maybe even an underwater swimming duck, nothing to worry about and probably harmless,' Tash was trying to convince the pair of them by conjuring up images of cute fluffy ducks and slowly dipped her paw carefully back in the water.

'Duck? Did you see the size of your *duck!* You could have made several thousand duck and Hoi Sin pancakes with the size of that duck, and now you've got me started on Chinese food I'm peckish...' said Fluke, his belly rumbling at the thought of some tasty crispy duck, cucumber, spring onion and Hoi Sin sauce pancakes, 'trust me Tash, that was no duck,' and watched as Tash took her paw out of the water and sat staring at her reflection.

'It's disappeared Fluke. We've been sat here several minutes now and not seen anything, so on the count of three we both start, OK?' looking at Fluke for confirmation.

'Right, on the count of three then,' and started a slow count – *'One; one and a half; two; two and a bit more; and three...!'* and they began slow methodical strokes and headed towards the shoreline.

'Of course you know why we've not seen the big creature, don't you Tash?' Fluke sniggered to himself.

'No, why's that Fluke?'

'Because an even bigger underwater dinosaur might have scared it off or eaten it!' shuddered Fluke, which caused Tash to start paddling furiously for the shoreline.

They were making slow progress but feeling confident of reaching dry land in a few minutes, when Fluke looked up and gasped out loud. 'Oh no Tash, quick, full reverse!' and started paddling backwards to slow them down.

'Whoa, what are you doing Fluke?' Tash looked up to see what the problem was, and instantly stopped her paddling, then gulped nervously, as there, stood on the shoreline, was a huge dinosaur staring straight at them. It had a huge long neck, massive body and really long tail.

'What now, Tash?'

Tash shook her head, 'Whatever we do it's bound to be a problem. Do we sit here on the lake with huge aquatic dinosaurs beneath us waiting for their lunch? Or do we paddle right up to that huge, hungry looking dinosaur stood waiting for its food order to be delivered?'

'Yep, either way we're going to be a takeaway!' laughed Fluke nervously, and they both shrugged. 'Here we go then Tash,' and ever so slowly they started to paddle towards the shoreline.

The volcano...

Papa and Mama Nummer were being carried underneath the two large flying reptiles. Several minutes of silence passed before either said anything, the initial shock of what had just happened finally passed.

'We'll be OK, just hold on tight and don't look down,' Papa said, trying to reassure Mama.

When somebody says *don't look down*, the first thing people do *is* actually look, and then regret it. 'We're high aren't we!' said Mama, 'and as for holding on tight, we don't have much of a choice. These reptiles have us in a strong vice like grip, I couldn't get free if I tried. Where do you think they're taking us?'

Papa looked all round and peeked down below. 'We're heading towards that smouldering volcano, so maybe these reptiles live nearby?'

'Oh, that's all right then...' joked Mama, 'a smoking volcano, trapped underneath two large flying dinosaurs and separated from Fluke and Tash, so nothing to worry about then!' Mama Nummer smiled.

'All in a day's work for Fluke and Tash I suppose, but this is all a bit new to us. I'm sure we'll be alright though,' Papa said confidently.

'So, pinch me to make sure this isn't a dream, but only an hour ago we were safely back home, just finished having our dinner and then hiding under the bed waiting for Fluke and Tash? Did you see what happened to them by the way, I hope they're safe?'

'I saw Fluke and Tash land in the lake, so they should be all right,' said Papa.

'I didn't think Fluke could swim that well? I guess he'll have to learn very quickly! Well, if nothing else, we've got some great aerial views, shame we don't have a camera,' replied Mama.

The reptiles closed in on the volcano and began circling around the crater top. The Nummers gazed down into the depths, which surprisingly had very little smoke coming out. They could feel the heat rising up to meet them, but again strangely it wasn't as hot as they both thought it might be, in fact it was a pleasant heat. The reptiles rode the hot air currents, circled twice more and then flew directly into the open crater. Reptiles and Nummers disappeared inside.

Amos the dinosaur lifeguard

'What now?' Whispered Tash. Having paddled as close to the shore as they dared, they sat on their floating case, bobbing around on a slight swell.

'Just a thought Tash, but have you actually tried starting the case to see if we can fly out of here?' Fluke whispered back.

'Dooh! Never thought of that,' Tash slapped her paw against her forehead and turned the handle three times. The case coughed and spluttered a few times, spun them around a little bit, but nothing really happened, and they were still sat near the shoreline with a huge dinosaur staring at them.

'Try it again Tash, it nearly worked!'

Tash turned the handle again, the case coughed and spluttered even more and still nothing.

'It doesn't sound too healthy does it Fluke, I think we've broken it!' said Tash shaking her head, 'I have a slight suspicion we've flooded the engine!'

'Errr, hi there, do you need a hand?' the large dinosaur shouted across to the pretend sailors, 'I've never actually rescued anybody before but always wanted to and you look like you could do with some help!'

Fluke looked at Tash and they both laughed. 'A dinosaur lifeguard! What would they say down at the local swimming club,' giggled Tash.

'Err, yeah that would be really kind of you,' Fluke shouted back, slightly bemused he was having a conversation with a dinosaur.

'My name's Amos,' the large dinosaur said, as he turned his massive body around to face the other way and began reversing back into the water, his long tail getting closer to the floating case. 'Climb up my tail and along my back and I'll carry you to dry land,' Amos instructed.

Fluke and Tash leapt from their case onto the large tail. Tash reached down and grabbed their magic suitcase and they both clambered to safety and sat on the broad back of Amos, who waddled out of the water and back onto dry land.

Fluke couldn't resist himself and slid down the long tail whooping with joy, and for a few seconds he pretended he was at a fun fair on a giant slide. Tash followed and slid down the tail, both now glad to be on solid ground.

They stood briefly staring back at the lake and watched in awe as a huge aquatic dinosaur leapt

from the lake, did a somersault, splashed back into the water and disappeared again.

'Whoa that was close, we were paddling there just a few minutes ago. I told you something big was swimming underneath us!' shivered Fluke, clearly in shock.

'Mosasaurus,' confirmed Amos.

'A what *a saurus*?' asked Tash.

'That dinosaur was called a Mosasaurus. They live in large lakes and in the oceans as well. They'll eat anything on and in the water, so luckily you're not still out there on the lake,' said Amos.

'Thank you Amos, you don't know how relieved we both are!' Tash said gratefully. 'Let us introduce ourselves, I'm Tash, my spotty friend over here is Fluke, and this...' she patted their suitcase with pride, 'is our magic time travelling suitcase,' and both Fluke and Tash explained where they had come from and some of the adventures they hoped to have.

Dinosaur Ants and spiders...

Nat hated ants, always had, even as a baby. He'd been careless when he was really young, and had only gone and slept in an ants nest one night! He didn't realise it was an ants nest until the morning when he had woken to find them crawling all over him, his body had been covered in little ant bites and it had hurt! His mum had scolded him, W*ell Nat, what do you expect, baby dinosaurs shouldn't sleep in an ants nest, it serves you right!*

So it was no surprise then that he loathed the sight and feel of them, and here they were, only this time they were huge. Hundreds of them scurrying around, a strange breed of soldier ant, so much larger than your average ant.

These soldier ants were only the guards. They worked for a strange creature that stood on two feet and was about nine foot tall. These were the real *slave masters* as he and the other young dinosaur slaves called them.

What he would give to see his mum, dad and friends again. He longed to hear his mum's voice telling him off. His mind drifted off to Amos, his best friend. I do hope Amos is OK — oh, the fun they had had playing dinosaur games.

'Why didn't I listen to my parents and the village elders...' he sighed, 'I just wanted to see what the volcano looked like close up.' It had been a game of dare. Each dinosaur would dare each other to see how close they could get before becoming afraid. Nobody actually thought for a second the rumours about missing and kidnapped dinosaurs would be true.

He was suddenly brought back to reality by one of the soldier ant guards giving Nat a prod and shove with its large sharp spear, shaped and sharpened exactly like one of its pincers and carved out of a large dinosaur bone. Mind you, he would rather be prodded with a spear than get bit by one of the ant's sharp pincers or mandibles, that had happened last week, and it really hurt!

Along with the ants were a breed of very large spider. The spiders worked alongside the soldier ants, and yet again were ruled by these strange two legged creatures. Each group of spiders and ants seemed to know exactly where to be and what job they had to carry out.

Nat looked down the line of friends he'd recently made. They were all young dinosaurs, tied together with a strong silky webbing that had been produced and spun by the spiders. It was nearly impossible to break. Everyone was being worked hard, digging and carrying, then more digging and more carrying.

The days were long and tiring, and Nat forgot how long he'd been down here in the depths of the volcano. It was strange though, you'd have thought being inside a volcano would be incredibly hot, but it wasn't too bad.

Nat had been told by one of his new slave friends, *Dice,* a Diceratops, how the volcano was formed in layers. There were different levels and the deeper underground you got, the hotter it was. Dice had even said he'd seen some huge underground lakes of fiery, red water bubbling near the very bottom of the volcano. Exactly where this fiery, red water went was a mystery, well a mystery to Nat, Dice and the rest of the gang. Dice had said there were hundreds of tunnels underneath them, all the tunnels snaked off into the sides of the mountain volcano and nobody knew where they led to.

The spiders made a type of huge carry sack, intricately spun using their super strong silky web and woven into a sack, which had been securely tied to each of the dinosaurs. As they moved together down the line, the sacks were filled with rocks and rubble which had been dug from the side walls of the volcano. Once the last dinosaur in the line had had his bags filled, they were marched off to empty the bags at some other point, then it all started again.

Nat looked up to the crater top. He liked to look up and see the sky, even though it was a long way off, just seeing the sky gave him hope. Hope that one day he and his friends could somehow escape. He watched as two Pteranodons flew into the crater. These two were different from the normal flying reptiles and were working in partnership with the ant colony. They appeared to be carrying two small creatures. Nat sighed, two more slaves were obviously being brought in, and already he felt sorry for the newcomers.

Map reading...

'We've got to find them Tash...' exclaimed an anxious Fluke, 'they're our friends and in trouble,' he continued.

'Of course we'll find them Fluke,' said Tash, equally worried.

'I'll help if I can,' offered Amos, shrugging his huge shoulders. 'I'm not sure how I can help but I'll try my best, although if they were taken to where I think they were taken....' His voice trailed off as he glanced nervously towards the volcano on the far horizon.

'Where do you think those two Pteranodons have taken our friends?' asked Tash, noticing Amos looking nervously into the distance.

'Nobody's really sure what's over there,' Amos nodded towards the smouldering volcano, 'but it's rumoured that's where missing dinosaurs get taken. They say there are strange creatures that kidnap you if you stray too close. We've had so many friends that have gone missing recently, never to be seen again,' he shivered at the thought, and was then interrupted by an almighty roar that ripped through the forest.

Fluke jumped and looked around nervously, 'What or who was that?' he asked Amos. Fluke's head turned in different directions trying to locate where the loud roar had come from.

'T-Rex...' Amos confirmed what they all feared the most, 'so we better move on quickly.'

'Which way, Amos?' asked Fluke scanning the horizon nervously.

'Well, if it was up to me Fluke, I'd head in the opposite direction from that roar!' joked Tash and began striding off, her satchel containing their maps, compass and binoculars slung rapidly over her shoulder.

Fluke rushed to join her, dragging the magic case, and fell into step, both having to walk fast to keep up with the lumbering Amos. They continued their fast walk for a few minutes until all three were happy they had left the T-Rex far behind.

'So why not get the map out to see where we're heading?' Fluke asked, slightly out of breath, leaning back against a giant redwood tree.

'Good idea Fluke,' said Tash, who'd also stopped to get her breath back, and looked up at the huge tree. 'These giant redwoods are massive Fluke,' she gasped, barely able to see the top branches.

'Fancy climbing that then?' joked Fluke also gazing up.

Tash dropped her satchel on the floor and opened the clasp. She delved inside and began rummaging around. Locating their map, she spread it on the forest floor and knelt down beside Fluke. 'We're here,' she pointed with her paw, 'and this volcano marked on the map must be the one that Papa and Mama Nummer were taken to.'

Tash had one last look at the map, folded it neatly and packed it away back in the satchel.

They stood, and readied themselves for their long hike.

'So how long will it take us to walk to the volcano then Tash?' Fluke asked.

'Well, if we had a large stride like Amos, not too long, but seeing as we've only got little legs I'd say a few days Fluke.'

Fluke who was stood in a shadow cast by their new large friend, shrugged and gazed up, 'so are you coming with us Amos?' he asked.

'Of course I'll go with you both. I never actually thought I'd say this, but I've secretly always wanted to go to the volcano.'

Nanotyrannus –
The tiny tyrant...

They were interrupted by a rustling coming from within the nearby bushes. Amos looked over and gasped as he spied a pair of faces peering at them through the ferns.

'*Quick, run*!' Amos fairly shouted out the warning, and not a second too soon either, as a pair of small but scary looking dinosaurs flew from the bushes and gave chase. 'Nanotyrannus, the tiny tyrants...' he shouted down to Fluke and Tash who were running beside Amos. 'They're related to the large T-Rex, and just as nasty,' Amos confirmed.

Now for a big dinosaur, Amos was remarkably quick and soon began to leave Fluke and Tash trailing behind. The Nanotyrannus sensed this and diverted their chase, leaving Amos to go crashing through the forest, and started to chase the easier option which just happened to be Fluke and Tash.

'Can dinosaurs climb trees Tash?' gasped Fluke.

'Can dogs?' puffed Tash, a little out of breath.

'If they're being chased by hungry Nanotyrannus then dogs can climb anything!' exclaimed Fluke.

'Right, that giant redwood up ahead, do you think you can climb it? Because we're only going to get one go at this Fluke, if we slip and slide down the tree we're in *big* trouble!'

Fluke raced past Tash and fairly ran up the first part of the large tree trunk until gravity began to take over and he started to slide back down. Thankfully the magic case had hooked itself onto a small branch, which allowed Fluke to gain a hold. He rested his paws on a small branch and gazed down at the two frustrated Nanotyrannus below, who were jumping up and down, snapping their powerful jaws together, desperate to reach their prey.

Tash sat next to Fluke on the same branch, and breathed a huge sigh of relief. 'Crikey Fluke...' she gasped, getting her breath back after the short chase, 'that was a close run thing. Hope Amos is OK, did you see where he went?'

'Didn't see him Tash, but I heard him crashing through the trees and ferns as he escaped. He might be a big fellow Tash, but my is he fast when he needs to be!' confirmed Fluke, who risked a quick glance down to the furious Nanotyrannus who were pacing up and down directly below their tree, just waiting for either Fluke or Tash to slip and fall.

'So, now what?' Tash muttered and turned to Fluke.

'Well, we can't stay up here all day, but then I don't fancy climbing down and trying to make friends with those two,' he pointed down to the Nanotyrannus who circled the tree and kept gazing up to the stranded Fluke and Tash. 'Is it my imagination Tash or are they licking their lips as if they're hungry?' gulped Fluke nervously.

Tash looked up, 'do you think you can climb a bit higher Fluke,' asked Tash.

'I don't think I can,' Fluke looked down and shivered, the thought of slipping and sliding down the tree trunk made him grip the branch even tighter than before.

Tash looked inside her satchel and began to rummage around, franticly trying to locate the length of rope she had noticed earlier.

'Phew, found it!' exclaimed Tash, breathing a sigh of relief. 'Don't move Fluke, I'll be back in a minute.'

'Don't move?' he laughed to himself, 'Where does she think I might go to...' Fluke joked with himself, glancing down. 'I'm hardly likely to pop down to the pet shop for treats, or wander off down the park for a walk, not with those two waiting for me to slip.'

He then looked back up to the rapidly disappearing Tash, watching in awe as she used her expert tree climbing skills. With a tinge of envy, Fluke wished he could climb trees as easily.

Tash climbed higher up the tree trunk and disappeared through a canopy of green needle like leaves, common for the redwood tree. They had to be a giant cousin of the conifer trees mum and dad had back home in the garden. Each tree branch seemed to be full of green needles and large bunches of cones weighed each branch down.

A few minutes of silence followed. Fluke couldn't hear anything above and he began to wonder what had happened.

Eventually a rustling could be heard from above and Fluke squinted as he tried to locate the source of the noise. A few stray cones fell, bounced of his head and continued their freefall downwards, only to be snapped up by the pair of eager Nanotyrannus, who then spat them out again as they didn't fancy cones for dinner.

Bird's nest hotel...

Tash scrambled easily back down the tree trunk. Her sharp claws were extended and dug deep into the tree bark as she re-joined Fluke on the branch he had been patiently waiting and hanging on to.

'Tie this length of rope around your waist Fluke and pull yourself up. I've tied the other end to a strong looking branch higher up. It will give us a bit more distance from those two,' she nodded downwards.

'What's up there Tash...' he asked as he checked to make sure the knot of the rope was securely fastened, 'and don't say tree branches!'

'I found some excellent sleeping arrangements for the night Fluke. We can rest up for the afternoon, get away from our two new admirers and gaze up at the stars tonight,' she chuckled and scrambled up the tree branch, looking over her shoulder as Fluke tugged the rope and began the steep climb.

Slowly but surely, Fluke followed the disappearing Tash up the tree trunk, and passing through the pine needles, he entered a new world.

High up near the top of the giant redwood the views were spectacular. The ground directly below had all but vanished from sight and thankfully so had the two Nanotyrannus.

Looking all round he saw a variety of trees, and many more giant redwoods, as far as the eye could see. From his new vantage point he saw deep rutted canyons that resembled *The Grand Canyon,* and the great smoking volcano in the distance they were meant to be heading towards. A huge tree lined canyon was full of water and had been turned into a great lake, which ran right up to the base of the volcano.

They both reached the largest bird's nest they had ever seen. Tash said gleefully 'here we are Fluke, our bed for the night!'

'Are you sure it's empty Tash, I mean we can't just knock and say "Hi there, we're on the run from two Nanotyrannus, so is it OK to stay for a while?"'

'It sounds empty Fluke, so I guess there's only one way to find out,' and Tash climbed over the edge and flopped into the nest, closely followed by Fluke. Just as he pulled himself over the edge, he heard Tash say, 'Oops! So, err, hi there, we're on the run from two Nanotyrannus ...' and Fluke came face-to-face with several baby Pteranodons, sat silently in their nest, just staring at the new arrivals.

Amos...

Realising he had managed to evade the two Nanotyrannus, Amos began to slow down, took in his bearings and noted with satisfaction he wasn't too far from home. Taking in great lungfuls of fresh clean mountain air, his shaking stopped as he calmed down, his thoughts turning to his two new friends.

Amos was in a dilemma – carry on back home and be safe and sound with his parents and the rest of the herd, or turn around and try to find Fluke and Tash. He made a decision and padded off. He'd need to let his parents know what had just happened, as they'd be worried about him.

He arrived safely back to the area that his herd had made temporary home. The herd were always moving from one area to another, never staying in one place for more than a few days. He spied his mum grazing on some vegetation, her long neck extended up to gracefully nibble on the leaves from a tall tree.

'And where have you been Amos...' his mum gazed down to her young son and carried on chomping the tasty leaves, 'you've been gone most of the day.'

'I've made some new friends Mum, two new visitors from a faraway land.'

'Really? A faraway land you say?' she gazed over the shoulder of Amos, trying to locate his new friends, 'so where are they then?' she queried, thinking that Amos was making up stories again, and carried on with her lunch.

'Well, that's the thing. We were chased by two Nanotyrannus and I lost them when we all ran to safety. Mum, I'd like to try and find them and make sure they're safe, I can't leave them out there on their own.'

'Talking of friends, *Tops* has been around looking for you,' she said between mouthfuls of food.

Another good friend of Amos', *Tops* was a Triceratops, the same age as Amos, and the three of them, Tops, Nat and Amos were always together. Their respective herds all seemed to travel in the same direction and at the same time, and after a while they had all become the best of friends. Sadly, with Nat missing, their gang had been reduced to just the two of them, himself and Tops.

'Tops was here?' Amos said happily, 'I'll go and find him then Mum, see you later,' and left his mum munching on more leaves and foliage.

'Tops will come with me to find Fluke and Tash,' he muttered to himself as he turned around and waddled off, 'and maybe we can head over to the volcano and find Nat, it would be great to get the gang back together,' thought Amos, then he shivered at the prospect of the long scary walk to the dreaded volcano, but Amos couldn't stand it if he didn't at least try to find Nat, Fluke and Tash.

Breakfast in bed...

Fluke had managed to haul himself over the edge of the nest and sat side-by-side next to Tash.

'I have a very important question,' he tapped Tash on the shoulder and whispered 'are we safe and do they bite?' They sat staring at the faces of the baby Pteranodons, their large beaks wide open as they started to make loud screeching noises.

Turning to face Fluke she said, 'well, I think we're safer up here than down there,' and pointed over the edge of the nest, 'these are only baby chicks, *big* baby chicks mind you, but without the sharp teeth of our not so welcome new friends down below.'

Fluke edged closer and calmly introduced themselves, 'so hi there, I'm Fluke and she's Tash, we hope you don't mind us joining you but we're on the run from two hungry dinosaurs with big sharp teeth,' and looked back to Tash, 'I don't think they understand me,' he sighed.

'Of course we understand you both,' one of the baby Pteranodons said, 'it's just that we don't get many visitors high up here in our nest, but I guess that's the point, high up here, safe and sound.'

'What's your name?' asked Tash, joining the conversation.

'Peter...' the baby chick replied and stretched his wings and started to flap them around as if trying to take off and fly around the nest, 'and we're waiting on our parents to come back with food,' he continued to flap his wings.

A shadow was cast over the nest causing Fluke to gaze upwards. He tapped Tash on the shoulder again, 'I think we have visitors,' and pointed to the two large reptiles hovering above their heads and about to land in the nest.

Fluke and Tash moved to the edge and watched as the parents landed and dished out the food they had caught. Fish was on the menu today as the baby chicks clamoured for attention for the catch of the day.

Once the food had been dished out, the hungry chicks stopped their squawking and peace was restored once again to the nest.

'Mum, Dad, meet Fluke and Tash, hope you don't mind them visiting but they're hiding up here for a while,' Peter introduced his two new friends.

'Hi there,' Fluke and Tash said together, 'and thank you for letting us stay,' added Tash.

'Of course we don't mind, you can stay for as long as you want,' the dad looked over to Fluke and Tash, 'but soon you'll be on your own as today is the day we leave the nest.'

'What? Today? I'm not ready Dad,' said Peter.

'Yes son, you've got to start flying soon. You're a Pteranodon don't forget, a flying reptile, not a land walking dinosaur.'

'But you know how I hate heights, and I don't think I'm ready to fly yet.'

'Oh don't be silly Peter,' his mother answered, 'you'll love it! Gracefully soaring high up looking down, using the air currents, it's so easy!' she added.

Flying lessons...

'What do you mean you don't like heights...' asked Fluke, 'I mean you're a bird aren't you?' and watched as the parents moved their chicks towards the edge of the nest, making them form an orderly line, with Peter at the back of the queue shaking nervously.

'Why does everybody assume that just because I've got wings I can fly and that I like heights,' Peter replied defensively.

The first chick leapt up and stood on the edge, stretched and flapped his wings and was given a gentle shove in the back from his dad. The baby chick dropped out of the nest and flew away using the air currents his mum had mentioned. He soared gracefully around and whooping with joy he shouted to his brothers and sisters, 'c'mon it's easy!'

The line was getting shorter as one-by-one all the baby chicks joined each other swooping and gliding around, until it was the turn of Peter.

He stood on the edge of the nest, his claws gripped the edge tightly and looked down, 'Oh, I really, really don't like heights,' he muttered.

'You can do it Son,' his mother whispered some encouragement, 'and more importantly you need to fly. Just flap your wings a bit like we showed you and join your brothers and sisters.'

'Son, you've got to do it,' his dad said sternly, 'it's time you flew the nest, besides we're all going now, we can't wait for you anymore.'

'I can't Dad, I'm scared of heights,' which was something you wouldn't normally hear a flying reptile say.

Peter's dad gave his son a gentle encouraging shove in the back, propelling him over the edge and watched as his son promptly disappeared from sight. His mum and dad took to the air and flew off with the rest of the family leaving a bewildered Fluke and Tash sat in the nest, which when empty, seemed huge.

'Well that's that then,' said Tash watching the family fly away, the baby chicks struggling to keep up.

'Help!' a scared voice from below could be heard.

Fluke looked over the edge and saw Peter hanging upside down, his sharp talons firmly gripping the underside of the nest. 'Whoa,' said Fluke in alarm, 'we thought you'd flown the nest. Wait right there, I'll be back in a second,' and turned to Tash, 'Peter's stuck, he needs our help.'

Tash was busy looking at their water damaged magic suitcase. She turned the handle to start it up, hoping it had dried out sufficiently to work. It coughed, spluttered and made some strange never before heard of noises but it was sort of running.

'Sounds like dad's old car at home,' joked Fluke.

'Hop on board Fluke, we're going to attempt a rescue!' and the pair clambered on. The case hovered and went over the edge of the nest. A clearly panic stricken Peter was beginning to lose his grip and was now hanging on with one talon, his spare wing frantically flapping trying to keep him airborne when thankfully help arrived, the magic case appeared, hovering underneath Peter.

'Just let go and we'll catch you,' instructed Fluke, and watched as Peter lost his grip and dropped onto the case nearly squashing captain Tash in the process.

The magic suitcase at this point cruelly decided it didn't want to be magic and didn't want to work properly again. It gave a huge cough, spluttered and started to drop, spinning wildly out of control.

'Not again,' muttered Fluke, covering his eyes with his paws, 'I'm getting dizzy and feel ill,' as the case spun and dropped like a stone.

Tash was frantically trying to get the case to start up again, and shouted out, 'Try flapping your wings, it might help save us.'

Now Tash had meant for Peter to flap his wings, so when she turned around and witnessed both Peter *and* Fluke flapping away, even in the dangerous predicament they found themselves in, she couldn't help but laugh. 'Well, I've seen it all now, "Is it a bird? Is it a plane? No it's *SuperFluke*, the world's first flying Dalmatian!" Next you'll be wearing a red cape and wear your underpants outside your trousers.'

Fluke saw the ground rushing towards them, stopped his flapping and covered his face with his paws. The case continued to plummet towards the ground...

Hotel Volcano...

The two rogue Pteranodons clutching Papa and Mama Nummer landed safely inside the volcano and were instantly surrounded by a large group of soldier ants, spiders and a huge ape-like creature that towered over everybody.

Papa Nummer shivered at the sight of their welcoming committee and then listened intently as the ape-like creature started talking in a strange dialect that Mama and Papa couldn't understand.

'Are you cold dear,' Mama Nummer chuckled, sensing her husband's discomfort.

'How can I be cold down here in a volcano? You know how I hate spiders...' he whispered back, 'it's always you that has to chase them from our tree stump home,' he admitted and shuddered again.

One of the spiders with strange body markings and huge hairy legs scuttled across the stony floor towards the Nummers. Its eight legs worked together to propel the hideous creature closer and closer until it stopped and studied both newcomers.

A strange and shrill click, clicking noise came from what Papa Nummer thought must its mouth. Papa looked over to Mama to see if she understood, who shrugged and said 'don't look at me dear, I don't speak the *spidersaurus* language.'

The spider turned around and whatever it said the soldier ant seemed to understand. He separated Papa and Mama to a certain distance and stood back, it held his long sharp spear, shaped and sharpened exactly like his very own pincers, one end clutched firmly in its legs and the other end propped on the floor.

Mama looked on in fascination as a powerful jet of silky thread shot straight from the *Spidersaurus* and watched as it began to coil up on the floor. When enough of the webbing had been produced, the soldier ant began tying it first to Papa and then Mama, binding them securely together.

Papa tested the strength of their new restraints and found them to be incredibly strong, they seemed unbreakable. 'Well, you're stuck with me a bit longer dear,' he joked to Mama, who grinned back and was about to speak when they were both prodded in the back by the ant's spear.

'Looks like were off then...' she sighed and followed her husband as they were led down a steep slope, joined together she had no option but to follow. 'Maybe we're being taken to the reception desk and be officially checked into *The 5 star Hotel Volcano*. I won't be recommending this hotel to friends mind you, and we certainly won't be tipping the staff here,' she joked, 'they're a bit rough with the guests!' She turned angrily to one of the ants who had prodded her roughly, causing Mama to stumble slightly.

Papa was looking all round at their new surroundings. Up above he could see the crater rim where they had entered, sunlight streaming through and shining brightly, tantalisingly close but far enough away to make escape very difficult.

They were heading downwards onto a rocky path that had been carved out of the granite face, each step took them further away from the outside world. Huge webs were strung everywhere, suspended between any gaps in the rock faces. Massive spiders sat resting in the centre of their webs, their beady eyes tracked the Nummers' journey. Huge rocky mounds could be spotted with ants streaming in and out, so that that was their captors sleeping arrangements sorted; webs and anthills.

Spiders and ants were everywhere. Those not resting were busy scurrying and scuttling around, obviously with a job to do and it seemed very little time to do it. To their left was the granite rock face and to their right on the far side of the volcano was a similar looking path carved into the rock that wound its way downwards into the dark depths. A huge cavernous chamber separated the two footpaths. He risked a peek over the edge and looked down, instantly wishing he hadn't as he couldn't see the bottom, their path and the one across the gaping chasm disappeared deep below.

Mama closed the gap and tapped Papa on the shoulder, 'what's that red glow down there?' she whispered and pointed over the edge, indicating the faint light they could just about see. Papa shrugged and carried on walking, being part-dragged and part-pushed by his captors. On the far side he saw a long line of young dinosaurs, all different types and ages, trussed together, they were shuffling along and prodded by their captors, heading down their own path.

The walked on. The deeper they got the warmer the air became, until they turned a corner and came upon a long line of similarly trussed up dinosaurs. The closest dinosaur turned around and smiled a friendly greeting to the Nummers. 'Saw you both arrive earlier,' he said, waiting patiently in line, 'my name's Nat and welcome to your new home, *The Volcano*,' he said sarcastically whilst glaring angrily at the soldier ants guarding them.

'I'm Papa Nummer and this...' he said turning around to indicate, 'is my wife.'

Mama Nummer smiled a friendly greeting and said 'Yes, we certainly arrived in style, our very own private flight especially laid on, a real 1st class service. So do you get many visitors here?'

'Sadly yes, more and more arriving every day,' Nat confirmed.

'What are all you dinosaurs doing here?' Papa asked the question.

'That's an interesting question and let me tell you what I think...' but Nat didn't get to finish as he was prodded by the ant with a sharp stick, the question was left unanswered for the time being. 'I'll tell you later tonight at dinner time, at least we all get fed well here, they have to keep our strength up as it's hard work,' and he turned back around, his captors leading him down the path.

Land of the giants...

Fluke sat there on the case for several seconds, eyes shut and paws covering his face. He slowly opened his eyes, breathed a huge sigh of relief and stepped down off the case onto a soft carpet of redwood pine needles.

Next to dismount was Tash, and finally Peter. They looked at each other and Tash burst out laughing, 'Well Peter, how was your first flying lesson?'

'I actually flew, I really did! OK, so it wasn't as graceful as mum and dad, but it was sort of flying, wasn't it?' he turned to Tash and Fluke for approval.

'You're wing flapping certainly slowed the case down which helped with a soft landing, it could have been so much worse!' confirmed Tash, who then turned to Fluke, 'what do you think Fluke?'

'I don't think dogs are meant to fly. My legs are aching after all that flapping,' he grinned, rubbing his aching leg muscles.

Peter stretched and flapped his wings, rose a few inches off the ground and landed again. He tried this three or four more times and gave up, 'well, maybe I need a bit more practice,' he looked bashfully at his two new friends.

Fluke was gazing around, glad to see the two Nanotyrannus had gone, obviously they'd got bored waiting for lunch.

They all heard a loud buzzing noise but couldn't locate where it was coming from. Spinning on the spot, they turned a full circle and there, in the distance, hovering between some strange looking flowers, was the biggest bee they'd ever seen.

'Have you noticed something Fluke?' asked Tash looking at their new surroundings.

'What do you mean?' said Fluke, scratching his ear.

'The size of everything. It's so big, everything is huge! Take Peter here, he's a bird, well technically a reptile, but still a type of bird and he's massive and still only a chick. That bee buzzing around the flowers is bigger than most birds at home, and those flowers are like mini trees!' she exclaimed.

Fluke nodded, 'you're right Tash...' he agreed, 'these redwood trees are giants,' and patted the sturdy tree trunk, 'those colourful mushrooms or toadstools are like houses, Amos was a large lump and don't get me started on the T-Rex or the Nanotyrannus.'

'Well, either we've shrunk since we got here or we've arrived in the *land of the giants*,' giggled Tash, who then proceeded to open the case.

'What are you looking for Tash?' asked Fluke, watching as she delved deep inside.

'We've got to get our bearings and head towards the volcano to find the Nummers,' she confirmed, as an assortment of items were being emptied from the case. Binoculars, rope, torch, compass… until finally she found what she'd been looking for, the map. Unfolding the large piece of parchment and opening it as far as she could, she spread it on the forest floor, smoothed the creases out and they all stood around gazing down.

'So we're about here, in the middle of a giant redwood forest,' Tash tapped the parchment with her paw and pointed to a spot on the map, 'and we've got to get all the way over to the volcano.'

'Oh an easy route march then!' Fluke said sarcastically. 'Just so as I understand correctly, to get to the volcano we've got to walk through this giant forest, probably being chased by hungry dinosaurs,' and then pointed to the map, 'cross over that dark brown patch on the map…'

'The swamp you mean…?' Tash interrupted, 'the dark brown patch is a swamp, Fluke.'

'Oh thanks. OK, that large swamp, and by the way you're not making this any easier Tash…' Fluke shook his head, muttered and then stared back down at the map, 'then we have to cross the slightly lighter brown patch, which is what if I dare ask?'

'Open plains, a big area of grassland or something similar,' Tash confirmed without glancing up from the map.

'Great! So a big open space with no hiding places, and then to the volcano,' Fluke finally finished.

Tash coughed, cleared her throat and said, 'well nearly, all except that blue area Fluke, you can't forget the blue area on the map, I mean it does sort of surround the volcano.'

'I know I'm going to regret asking, so please tell me that blue bit isn't what I think it is?' He looked up hopefully, but the look said it all, 'OK, so it's water, my favourite! I can't swim and it's probably filled with huge dinosaurs swimming in it just waiting for me to dip my paws into the water.'

'So nothing to worry about then...' laughed Tash, 'just an average day in the life of a Fluke and Tash adventure!'

Amos and Tops...

'The volcano? Are you crazy?' said Tops, who stopped his lumbering walk and turned to stare at his friend, 'you're kidding me, right?' suddenly convinced his best friend had gone mad or, as he hoped, was only joking.

Amos had found Tops' heard of Triceratops and sought out his friend. The pair had walked off together to find a fresh patch of vegetation to munch on.

'No, I'm not crazy Tops, Nat's there, I'm sure of it. And Fluke and Tash will be trying to find their two friends, the Nummers.'

'Fluke and Tash? The two you rescued from the lake? Wish I'd been there to see that,' he chuckled. 'So you really think Nat's been kidnapped and is being held prisoner in the volcano?'

'I saw it with my own eyes. Those two Pteranodons snatched the Nummers and flew off heading in the direction of the volcano. The rumours are true Tops, I know they are. Where else are all the missing dinosaurs and our friends being taken? I mean they can't all vanish into thin air!'

Tops went quite, deep in thought. 'It'll take us at least two days of walking Amos, you do know that, right? And we'll need to let our parents know.'

'I've already told mine,' Amos confirmed, 'c'mon, your parents are over there. Let's do this and get started before I change my mind. Nat needs us!' and the pair sauntered off, wondering what they had let themselves in for.

The long trek...

Fluke took the binoculars and looped them over his head using the carry strap, Tash folded up the map and Peter took control of the compass, the rest of the items were stored carefully back in the case.

'So what's this then?' Peter asked with a confused look on his face staring down at the shiny gold compass, turning it around in his talons. He was fascinated by the needle that always seemed to point straight ahead no matter which way he turned the case, and the symbols N, NE, E, SE, S, SW, W, NW that were etched in gold around the outside face of the case.

'That my friend, is going to help us locate the volcano, and with a bit of luck, hopefully you're mum, dad, brothers and sisters as well,' said Fluke.

'Why do we need it? I can see the top of the volcano, it's over there, look!' Peter replied and pointed with his wing.

Tash chuckled, 'good point Peter, but what happens when it's dark, or what happens if you're deep in a forest...'

'Which we're going to be, in a few minutes,' interrupted Fluke.

'As I said, deep in the forest?' said Tash, 'or at any other time you can't see it,' Tash continued, 'the needle always points north and to get to the volcano we need to head north.'

'Wow, that's magic!' gasped Peter and held the compass, gazing down at this wondrous gadget.

Tash grabbed hold of the magic case and had one last look around to make sure they'd packed everything. 'So Peter, follow the needle and let the long trek begin!' They bunched together; Fluke to the left, Tash to the right with Peter in the middle, all holding each other's paws and wings. The three new friends headed off, Fluke and Tash desperate to find the Nummers, and Peter hoping to be re-united with his family.

Fluke began whistling the theme tune from another of his favourite films, *The Wizard of Oz*, with Tash changing the wording, she began to sing 'We're off to find the Nummers, the wonderful Nummers from home...' but was interrupted by Fluke, 'and you said I can't sing?' he laughed.

The banter continued, anything to keep up the bravado as they were all nervous. Night was drawing in, the path they were following steered them through thick forest vegetation and weaved between the trunks of the giant redwoods and huge ferns that grew everywhere.

Peter lost sight of the volcano and started to panic until Tash reminded him of the compass. They stopped for a few seconds and studied the spinning needle in the fading light, got their bearings and changed direction. Their new course took them off the easy path and forced them to hike through even thicker foliage, tree vines and other obstacles. It was hard work and progress was slow.

They entered a clearing and decided to sit out the night there, darkness was drawing in rapidly and it was agreed to make camp and wait for morning before continuing.

'Feels just like Sherwood Forest, doesn't it,' reminisced Fluke. 'Remember we made a few camps in the forest, didn't we Tash?'

'Yeah, but the only danger we faced then was an angry Friar Tuck who's picnic you *borrowed*. Here we've got a hungry T-Rex and all sorts,' Tash answered, whilst busily using some fallen tree branches and large fern leaves to make a make shift shelter for the night.

Shhh, did you hear that...?

Several more minutes passed with Fluke handing Tash an assortment of tree branches, whilst Peter helped Tash construct the frame. They stood back to admire their handiwork.

'You're pretty useful at camp-making Peter, so how did you learn to build like that?' asked Tash.

'Instinct really,' he shrugged, 'mum and dad built our nest at home, I'm guessing it's what us Pteranodons just do, build nests. Although I've never slept on the ground before, it's always been high up in the trees.'

'Just as well we're on the ground Peter, you don't like heights, remember!' joked Fluke.

'Yeah, and you don't like climbing trees Fluke,' laughed Tash.

They nestled down for the night, nice and snug in their new tent, when a thought struck Tash. She leant across to Fluke and rested her paw on his forehead.

'What are you doing?' he asked and shoved her paw away.

'Just checking your temperature Fluke. Are you feeling OK? A bit unwell, a slight fever maybe?' she asked trying to keep a straight face.

'Why? What are you getting at?' replied Fluke, even more confused.

'Food Fluke, you've hardly mentioned food since we've been here, so I thought you must be ill!' she joked.

'Haha, very funny Tash,' he shook his head, grinned and then said, 'OK, so what are we going to eat?'

Tash rummaged in her satchel and laid out some tins of tuna and a packet of dog biscuits. 'Provisions Fluke, thought I'd better pack something.'

'What's Tuna?' asked Peter.

'Fish,' replied Tash and watched in dismay as Peter lunged forward and gobbled down one of the shiny tins of tuna.

'Doesn't taste like fish,' complained Peter.

'Err, you meant to take it out of the tin first,' laughed Fluke, as he proceeded to open one of the tins and watch as Tash and Peter shared their meal.

Fluke turned his attention to some tasty dog biscuits, ripped open the packet and devoured half its contents. He slumped back on the floor, burped, and said, 'I feel full and sleepy now. We've had an interesting day, wouldn't you say?'

'A busy day!' Tash replied, 'I think we'd better get some sleep and rest up, we've got another big day tomorrow,' and with that all three campmates rolled over and fell into a deep sleep.

Two hours later Tash woke with a start. She sat bolt upright and looked around their tent, noticing Fluke was also wide awake.

Fluke started to speak but was cut off before he could say too much. 'Shhh, did you hear that?' whispered Tash.

'I was about to say that something woke me up,' he whispered back, when another loud crashing noise shattered the silence. Something very large was getting closer and heading directly towards their tent...

Digging...

Papa had been given a basic tool to work with. Holding the instrument in his hands, Papa studied it, shrugged and turned to Mama, 'It's like a basic pickaxe,' he whispered, 'how have the ants and spiders invented these? We always thought mankind invented tools in the Stone Age era, but that's many, many years in the future.' The pickaxe head was made from hard bone and tied firmly to a wooden handle with the strong but flexible webbing spun from the spiders.

'Well, who do you think is in overall charge down here? It's certainly not the ants and spiders is it, they're just working for the two legged ape-like creature we've seen. Do they remind you of anyone?' asked Mama.

Papa wracked his brain and suddenly it dawned on him, 'Of course, how could I have missed the likeness. It's a *Bigfoot* or *Sasquatch* isn't it?' said Papa. 'Well, certainly a *Bigfoot* lookalike. I know scientists say they can't prove they exist, and that they're a hoax or just folklore, but *Bigfoot* was meant to live in North America.'

Papa was forced to join a long line of prisoners and made to dig into the lava rock walls, whilst Mama stood behind him and was made to shovel the debris into the sacks carried by the big dinosaurs. This process went on for what seemed like hours; dig, shovel, dig and shovel some more. Every time anybody rested for a while they got a prod from one of the ants and were made to dig faster.

Papa looked down the long line and spotted Nat. He was one of the larger dinosaurs being used to cart the sacks away. Nat didn't dare talk but nodded a greeting, Papa watched as his last bag was filled and Nat was escorted away, returning several minutes later.

At the end of the shift, the ants and spiders communicated with each other in that now familiar click, clicking sound. The ants came around, took away the pickaxe handles and led Papa and Mama away to join another line. This time Nat was in front of them and he managed a few words.

Underground city...

'So how was your first day?' Nat asked.

'Painful,' said Papa through clenched teeth. 'It's hard work, my back aches and is really sore,' he said and began to massage his aching muscles.

'So what's this all about...,' Mama pointed to the dinosaur prisoners, ants, spiders and the *Bigfoot* type creature that was watching everything. 'What is actually happening down here?'

'Where do I start...' sighed Nat.

'At the beginning?' offered Mama. 'If we're going to help and plan an escape we need to understand everything that's going on.'

'Well, we're all here to help build a huge underground city for these horrid creatures...' he pointed angrily to a watching *Bigfoot*.

'An underground city?' replied a surprised Papa who looked towards Mama.

'Kind of makes sense really,' she replied deep in thought. 'Below ground they'd be a lot safer, an impenetrable city.' She nodded in awe, 'very intelligent thinking, kind of like our tree stump at home when you think about it, miles upon miles of underground tunnels and nobody knows we live down there.'

'So what happens with the rocks you cart away?' asked Papa curiously.

'They're taken to an area and crushed down into dust, which is then taken to the surface and scattered onto the ground, but we don't know why,' Nat shrugged.

The line they were in was shuffling forward. 'So what's happening now?' asked Papa turning to Nat, changing the subject.

'Lunchtime, and I'm hungry,' confirmed Nat.

The line they were in reached the front. Bowls of a green liquid were being handed out. Mama sniffed the contents. 'Smells like a kind of vegetable stew,' she said and tipped the bowl to drink the contents, 'and it tastes good.'

'Not as good as your cooking dearest,' said Papa who had cleaned his bowl, wiping his finger round the rim, not wishing to leave anything behind.

'So I assume they grow the vegetables outside on the sides of the volcano?' asked Mama deep in thought.

'Yes, I suppose so,' said Nat, greedily drinking his stew, 'Why do you ask?'

'It's making a bit more sense now,' said Mama. 'Crushed volcanic rock is full of minerals which when mixed with soil makes the ground very fertile. Combine the good growing soil and the warmth from the volcano and hey presto you've got ideal growing conditions. Ingenious, I'm very impressed,' said Mama.

'But why grow anything?' asked a slightly confused Papa.

'To keep the workers fed, so they stay strong and keep working. There's loads to this volcano we've not seen yet, for instance where is this city they're building? This...' she pointed around them, 'is only the top of the volcano, the city must be deeper underground.'

'It is deeper. My friend Dice has been down there. He says there's some kind of red, fiery water bubbling away down there...' Nat pointed over the edge, 'and huge buildings are being built using specially shaped building blocks.'

'Red, fiery water? That sounds like the lava flow, or to be precise, Magma flow,' confirmed Papa.

'We need to escape tonight and see what's really going on,' whispered Mama.

'If I can manage to get these knots untied we can have a scout around,' said Papa.

'If you get the knots untied you can get out and be free. Don't hang around here,' said Nat looking all around in case they were being overheard.

'We'd never abandon you all,' Papa said.

Mama continued where Papa had left off and pointed to all the tethered baby dinosaurs, 'we're all leaving here together Nat, trust us on that. Besides, we've got to wait for Fluke and Tash, they'll be here soon, I just know they will.'

That was close...

Tash opened her satchel and quickly retrieved the torch. Using the switch on the side she attempted to turn it on, but nothing happened.

'Give it here,' whispered Fluke and took the torch, and banged it against his paw as he'd seen dad do on several occasions when the batteries were running low. The torch sprung into life, a powerful beam of light filled the tent, dazzling Tash.

'Whoa, point it the other way, not at me!' she said and watched as Fluke spun around and pointed the light at the entrance of the tent.

The loud noises stopped, just inches away. Tash could hear someone or something breathing and noticed the tent bulge as something prodded the walls from outside.

'Take a look outside Fluke,' whispered Tash.

'Me? Why me?' Fluke complained.

'You've got the torch, that's why!' replied Tash and shoved Fluke in the back, propelling him closer to the entrance.

Tash joined Fluke, the pair stood side-by-side. Turning round she saw Peter was still blissfully unaware they had visitors, as he was still fast asleep.

'On the count of three, we'll both take a peek outside,' confirmed Tash. 'Ready? One, two and three...' they drew back the makeshift tent door and Fluke shone his torch outside. Two things happened simultaneously. Firstly, the torch shone directly into a huge, bony, three-horned face. The sudden bright light caused the newcomer to fall backwards in shock. Secondly, the surprise of seeing a huge, bony, three-horned face at their tent entrance caused Fluke and Tash to shout out in alarm and tumble backwards, tripping over Peter in the process and waking him up.

'Let's get out of here!' said Fluke preparing to evacuate the tent, rapidly turning off the torch as it told whoever was outside exactly where they were.

With the light now extinguished, it became pitch black in the tent. Tash packed her belongings into the satchel and turned to flee out the front but ran into Fluke who was preparing to leave the tent by the rear. They collided and fell into a heap on the floor and in the process sat on Peter who was just standing up. The tent walls couldn't take any more and began to collapse all around them, leaving all three sat on the floor in the middle of a pile of tree branches and fern leaves.

In the chaos, Fluke had dropped the torch on the floor. It now decided to turn itself back on, shining brightly into two huge startled faces.

'Fluke, Tash? Is that really you?' one of the two large faces said.

'Amos? Oh are we glad to see you. We wondered who it was outside the tent. You had us a bit worried there for a few seconds,' Tash breathed a huge sigh of relief.

'A bit worried?' laughed Fluke, 'petrified more like,' said Fluke, 'I thought our two friends the Nanotyrannuses had found us again!'

'This is Peter, he's joined us on our trip to the volcano,' said Tash and made the introductions. Peter stood, unfurled his wings, flapped them a bit and said hello.

'Oh and this is my best friend Tops,' said Amos pointing to the triceratops.

Tops moved in closer, looked all round and whispered nervously, 'did you say Nanotyrannuses?'

'Yes, but that was ages ago, they're long gone now,' confirmed Fluke. 'And can I say what an impressive set of horns you have there. It's enough to scare anybody in daylight, but deep in the woods late at night it certainly made us jump!'

'That was close you know,' said Tash, 'we heard something crashing through the bushes and thought our tent would be squashed with us still in it.'

'Tops here is a bit clumsy, if it hadn't been for the bright shining light, we probably would have gone straight through your tent and not even known you were there,' said Amos, 'but I'm so glad that we've found you both.'

Time to explore...

It had been a long day and all was quiet in the sleeping zone. Dinosaurs were resting and the ant guards meant to be keeping watch over them were dozing. Papa and Mama had eventually managed to free themselves. Papa looked over to Nat, who was watching with interest.

A whispered conversation took place, 'Nat, we're going to investigate but we promise we'll be back soon.'

'OK, but take care. If they find you wandering around at night on your own you'll get into big trouble,' said Nat, deeply concerned.

'Don't you worry Nat, we've plenty of practice at creeping around undetected,' confirmed Mama, and with that they crept away silently, keeping close to the rock walls, always watching and listening.

The Nummers made their way down the rocky path, passing large spiders resting in the centre of their huge webs. Thankfully the Nummers were small and very, very, quiet. The guards would have to look long and hard and have super hearing to detect their progress.

'It's weird down here,' whispered Mama, 'during the day it's a hive of activity but at night it's peace and calm, you'd never believe we were in the same place.'

They were rounding a long bend in the lava rock walls where an endless amount of side tunnels disappeared off into the gloom. They could only guess as to where they all led. They kept following the main path downwards. Papa noticed the further they went the warmer it became, but surprisingly, considering they were in a volcano, it was a pleasant heat. They looked up and noticed large holes in the rock ceiling which seemed to lead all the way to the surface. Mama thought they were possibly ventilation holes to let fresh air in and let some of the heat out. The bend in the wall straightened out and they came to a sudden full stop.

A ledge which overlooked a spacious cavern was directly in front of them. Steps on either side had been carved into the rock floor leading down to the cavern below.

Stepping up to the edge, they carefully peered over and gasped as they looked down onto a huge building site. The city that Nat had mentioned was under construction, but no activity was taking place right now, the building site was as quiet as the rest of the volcano.

'So here we are then,' muttered Mama, 'the underground city. The reason these poor dinosaurs have been kidnapped, slave labour to help this *Bigfoot tribe* construct an underground fortress.'

Papa started to walk down the steps as he needed to get a closer look. Mama followed, spinning around to make sure they were alone.

'I can't believe there aren't any guards here,' he whispered.

'Why would there be? Nobody has ever been able to escape their shackles and have a look.'

'I guess they didn't bank on having some nosy Nummers here then,' chuckled Papa.

It's that way...

The group was getting bigger; Fluke, Tash, Peter, and now Amos and Tops. They had waited till sunrise, tidied up their messy camp, made plans and generally readied themselves for a new day.

'So it's agreed then?' asked Tash, 'we're all heading to the volcano. Me and Fluke to find the Nummers, Amos and Tops to find Nat, and Peter to hopefully be re-united with his family.'

Peter nodded his agreement and took it upon himself to lead from the front, striding off into the forest. The rest stood still and watched him disappear, counted to ten, and watched in amusement as he scuttled back having realised he was headed in the wrong direction.

'I had the compass upside down,' he said bashfully, turning his shiny new gadget around and waiting for the needle to settle down. 'It's that way,' he pointed with his wing and strode off, this time in the right direction.

The going was hard, chopping their way through thick vines and vegetation. Peter lost sight of the volcano top and stopped every ten minutes to check his new toy, the compass, to make sure they were still headed in the right direction. Even Amos, who stood so much taller than everybody else, couldn't see the volcano anymore. Most of the morning had gone before they began to see the edge of the forest.

The small group collectively breathed a huge sigh of relief as they had successfully completed the first part of the journey. It was agreed to rest for a while on the outskirts of the forest, collect their thoughts and have a spot of lunch.

Tash rummaged in the satchel for food; Tuna for herself and dog biscuits for Fluke. Amos and Tops found a branch full of fresh leaves to chomp on, whilst Peter decided he would try and catch some fish from the large river that ran alongside the path they were on.

Fluke and Tash watched in amusement as Peter sat on the river bank, wings folded, his beady eyes following some tasty looking fish that were swimming past. Every time he plunged his beak into the water to try and catch one, the fish always managed to escape being caught. Peter could only hold his breath for a few seconds and repeatedly came up for air without a single fish.

'How do mum and dad do this,' he muttered, closed his eyes and plunged his head underwater, again he surfaced without catching a single thing.

Fly fishing for beginners...

Tash felt sorry for Peter, as despite his best efforts he was getting frustrated and clearly getting hungry.

'Do you want a hand Peter?' she offered.

Peter nodded, a puddle of water surrounded him, dripping from his head as he was getting drenched, and he needed some food.

Tash looked around and spied a long knobbly stick laying nearby on the ground. She dragged the stick over to the edge of the forest and grabbed a pawful of vine. Giving it a tug she pulled it free and tied it to the top end of the stick.

Looking around she saw Fluke laid out on the grass resting and occasionally flapping his paw to shoo away an annoying fly that buzzed around his head. He sat upright as the annoying insect was making a nuisance and he managed to catch the critter in his paw.

'Gotcha!' he said triumphantly.

Before Fluke released it Tash said, 'don't let the fly go Fluke, tie it to this long length of vine, I've got an idea.'

'Tie it to the vine?' he queried, 'why, are you making it a lead and taking it for a walk?' he chuckled.

'A fishing rod Fluke, time to catch some dinner,' grinned Tash.

She watched as Fluke tied some of the vine around the fly and then scanned the ground for the last item she needed. There, lying on the ground, was a prickly thorn which Amos had pulled down from one of the branches. 'That'll do nicely,' she grinned, 'a makeshift fishing hook,' and tied the thorn to the end of the line just below the fly.

'What's that?' asked a quizzical looking Peter, watching Fluke and Tash walk over to the water's edge wielding a long stick with a long length of vine attached.

'Apparently it's a fishing rod. Tash is trying to catch us some dinner,' said Fluke, 'although we've not fished before, Tash here is attempting to become a master fisherman,' he laughed and watched with interest as Tash stood on the banks of the stream and cast her line into the water.

Tash waited patiently, her new rod resting in her paw, the fishing line, hook and a tasty, tempting fly reached right to the middle of the river. Five minutes had passed and she pulled the line out of the water to check the hook was still in place.

'Caught anything yet?' asked Fluke.

'Patience Fluke, fishing is all about being patient,' she whispered, 'and also being quiet, you don't want to scare the fish away,' she said, staring at Fluke, who got the hint and wondered off.

Catch it...

Fluke was bored. He began wandering up and down the bank and kicked a flat stone with his paw. Reaching down he picked it up and wondered how far he could skim it across the water. Releasing the stone he watched as it hop-scotched and skimmed across the surface before finally sinking below the water line. 'Not bad,' he said to himself.

'You can be really annoying at times,' said Tash shaking her head, 'I'm trying to catch some fish and you're messing around scaring them away.'

'You're not going to catch anything with that homemade rod anyway,' he laughed and picked up another flat stone.

A few more minutes and skimmed stones later, Fluke was about to try and beat his previous record of stone skimming when he heard a shout. Turning around he watched in disbelief as Tash was evidently struggling with something large, and began slipping and sliding towards the water's edge.

'Quick, give me a hand, we've got something big on the end of the line,' she was shouting for help to Fluke, Peter and anyone else who was listening.

94

Amos and Tops joined Fluke and Peter on the river bank. 'What have you caught?' asked Peter, the excitement evident in his voice.

'Probably a discarded shopping trolley,' said Fluke jokingly, joining the spectators on the river bank 'that's all we have in our river back home.'

Tops stood behind Tash and helped by holding the rod, and on the count of three they both pulled together.

To say Fluke was shocked would be an understatement. As the rod was pulled back he watched in awe as a huge silvery fish came flying out of the water, fell off the hook and was headed directly towards him.

'Quick, catch it,' shouted Tash as she watched the fish fly over her head. Turning around she saw Fluke drop his stone and stood there, eyes shut and paws extended ready to catch dinner.

It landed in Fluke's outstretched paws and as he tried to grab hold it starting wriggling. Fish being fish, it was incredibly slippery, so it was no surprise when it slipped out of Fluke's paws, dropped to the floor and started to wriggle back towards the water's edge.

'Don't lose it Fluke,' shouted Tash.

'It's like trying to catch a wet bar of soap,' complained Fluke and began to chase it before it reached the water. He pounced, grabbed hold and started a wrestling match, which the fish seemed to be winning!

The tasty morsel wriggled free yet again, and landed closer to the water's edge. Desperate to catch it, and without thinking, Fluke did the unthinkable. He waded into the water and grabbed hold of its tail, this time he successfully held on, and triumphantly stood knee-deep holding his prize aloft. He threw the fish back onto the river bank, which was then rescued by Tash and Peter who dragged it back onto dry land, their dinner for the night was safely secured.

Realising he was actually in deep water, Fluke was desperate to get out and started to wade ashore. Not being able to see the bottom of the river and in his haste to get out, his paws slipped on some stones. He fell backwards and unable to regain his balance went completely underwater. Drenched, he stood back up, water streaming from his wet clothes.

'Thanks Fluke, we've got some tasty fish for dinner,' said Peter.

'We have, have we? I don't even like fish!' moaned Fluke, dripping wet as he made his way back to dry land, 'and I hate water even more!'

Fluke eventually dried out and dinner was served. Tash had made a small campfire using dried kindling and a fire starting method she'd learnt back in Sherwood Forest. The fish was descaled, and cooked over the open fire. Licking his lips Fluke was picking at the fish bones.

'Didn't think you liked Fish,' Tash laughed.

'Well, as I saved the day I thought I'd better try some and it was rather tasty. It just needs a bit of salt, vinegar and chips to go with it,' he joked.

Swamp monster...

A large beady eye on a huge sinewy periscope popped up through the grunge, swivelled around looking for victims and disappeared from sight again. It was hungry, not having had any visitors for many days now. It swam below in the gloom of the swamp, it was the only creature capable of such a feat. Its many long tentacles helped pull it through the slime as it travelled beneath; waiting, waiting...

The swamp covered a huge area. It had hundreds upon hundreds of little sandbank mounds. Small islands of safety dotted here and there, very similar to stepping stones across a stream, forming a path through the middle to the far side and safety.

Surrounding each small island was the actual swamp. A bubbling gloop of sticky brown liquid, which clung to your body making swimming impossible. Everything avoided the swamp if possible, many a dinosaur had braved the crossing, but very few made it across successfully.

Anybody foolish enough to attempt a crossing would have to jump from mound to mound. There was only one direct route through and if you knew the correct path you could jump from one to another no problem, but if you took the wrong route you'd be stuck in the maze of islands for days getting hopelessly lost.

If you fell off a sandbank into the gloop you'd struggle to get out again as the thick soup-like substance dragged you down until you disappeared from sight, never to be seen again.

Those vines look alive...

The intrepid explorers had fed well on their fish dinner, and Amos and Tops had stripped one of the trees bare of its vegetation. The party of five were full of food and now fully rested. It was time to move out, they couldn't put it off any longer. The volcano rim was sighted, Peter used his compass, got their new bearings and the group headed off.

Tash was striding alongside Amos, talking about life living in a herd of dinosaurs, moving from place-to-place, and the conversation got round to his friend Nat.

'If he's there in the volcano we'll find him Amos, I promise,' assured Tash.

Fluke was walking with Tops and Peter, who kept attempting to fly by flapping his mighty wings but still couldn't take off for more than a few seconds and even then only managed to get a couple of inches off the ground. 'You'll fly one day Peter,' he said, 'it takes time to be a fully grown Pteranodon, don't be in a rush to grow up.'

The giant redwood trees in this part of the forest were covered in vines and creepers and they had to hack their way through. Reaching another clearing, Fluke rested a while. 'How much further until we reach the end of this part of the forest Tash?' Fluke asked, huffing and puffing, clearly out of breath.

Tash got the map out, laid it on the floor and studied it. 'Not far Fluke, we're here and the edge is only there,' she pointed to the dark brown area.

'Oh yeah, the swamp, what joy,' Fluke grimaced, 'I'm so looking forward...' and was about to say more when he was stopped mid-sentence.

Tops noticed Fluke staring, his gaze took him behind Tash. 'What's wrong Fluke, you look startled?' he asked.

'Those vines are like tentacles and they're moving,' Fluke whispered, his stare not leaving the tree behind Tash, who'd looked up from her map reading. 'I'm not imagining it, they were moving, honestly,' he confirmed.

'What do you mean, moving? You must have got a water logged brain after your swim in the river Fluke. How can vines move? It must be the wind,' said Tash, but suddenly she didn't feel overly confident with her explanation and shuddered.

Tash had begun to pack away the map when she saw a flicker of movement out of the corner of her eye. She looked down and noticed a long vine had snaked along the ground between her paws. A shouted warning of panic came from one of the group.

They were surrounded. It was like having a huge octopus with hundreds of tentacles creeping across the forest floor, moving and almost sniffing the air, as if they could only detect by scent and not sight. The creeping vines felt their way along the ground, rapidly moving closer and closer.

Fluke started jumping up and down, stamping on the vine closest to him. His antics caused a shriek from something back behind the bushes, and then Fluke himself suddenly yelped in alarm and watched in horror as a creeping vine begin to coil itself around one of his paws and work its way up his leg ...

Building inspectors...

The Nummers crept quietly down one set of steps, and headed toward the huge building site down below. After all the noise of the day the silence that surrounded them felt odd.

'Look at the scale of those walls Mama, they're impressive and very tall,' said Papa craning his neck to see the top.

Approaching one of the walls, Mama ran her hands up and down a building block and studied it closely. 'They fit snuggly together,' she noticed. 'How on earth have they managed to shape them so accurately? They don't have stonemasons around, so how? I need to find out,' she muttered in wonderment.

They strolled around the whole structure, walking past a few entrances and eventually decided to pop their heads in a doorway to have a look. The same could be said for the inside. Impressive walls had been built with a maze of tunnels seemingly leading to the centre.

'Big rooms for big creatures. I assume the whole ant colony would live nearby as well, so they can be ready whenever *Bigfoot* commands them,' said Mama.

'What about the spiders?' Papa asked.

'Look around dear. The walls are so huge, I guess they'll spin their webs high up off the ground, like they do at home,' she added and watched Papa shiver as he didn't much care for spiders, especially large ones like these.

They left the inside of the underground city and began to follow another path which lead them around another corner. The deeper underground they went, the faint red glow they noticed earlier was getting brighter. The heat was rising too.

They walked into another huge cavern and gasped as they witnessed a river of fiery red liquid passing through. The magma flow was a river of flowing molten rock direct from the earth's core. Papa tapped Mama on the shoulder and shushed her. There was plenty of activity here.

Several of the *Bigfoot* creatures were issuing instructions to the soldier ants and spiders, who in turn were stood around a group of slave dinosaurs and issuing instructions. This was obviously where the night shift workers were.

'What are they doing?' whispered Mama, mesmerized by the whole spectacle, watching closely.

'They've got some sort of large bucket attached to a winch and pulley system, dipping it into the lava flow, scooping it up, swinging the winch around and pouring it onto the ground. Why, I don't know, but we need to get a better look,' he replied and began to edge a bit closer to the small group.

Concealing themselves securely behind a rock, Mama said 'they're not just tipping the molten lava on the floor, they're filling specially made moulds, look!' Mama and Papa watched as the winch swung around and poured the contents of its bucket into a building block shaped mould.

Instantly the hot lava began to cool. The cooling process would take many hours, but would soon produce a building block, the building blocks to form the new underground city walls.

Papa was intrigued by the whole spectacle. He felt a tap on his right shoulder and turned his head to ask Mama what she wanted, and was surprised she wasn't there. Realising a bit too slowly that Mama was actually knelt on his left hand side he spun round to look behind. Four stern faced soldier ants glared back angrily, their long spears were pointing directly at the two spies.

'Ooops...' muttered Papa, as Mama also spun around, 'I think we've been caught in the act,' and they raised their hands in surrender to be led away.

Nobody move...

'OK, nobody move a muscle. We'll be safe if we don't move!' shouted Amos, and much to everybody's surprise, the vines suddenly stopped their advance.

'I couldn't even if I tried,' complained Fluke, who was bound securely by the creeping vine. It had started to wrap itself around his paw and then gradually worked its way up his leg.

Fluke glanced over to his friends and noticed that typically he was the only one entangled by the vines. *Why is it always me, he thought*, then spoke out loud, 'so now what? I mean you say we can't move, fine, but we can't stay here all night long. Any suggestions?' Fluke glanced around to his friends hoping one of them had a great plan.

'Panic and run?' joked Peter.

'We've heard about these vines haven't we Tops?' who nodded in agreement and let Amos continue. 'The vines are triggered by movement, the main carnivorous plant is back there, hidden in the undergrowth somewhere. The vines stretch out to capture anything that moves and it drags its prey back to the body to be eaten...,' his voice trailed off as he realised he shouldn't have told Fluke this bit of disturbing news.

'Eaten?' gulped Fluke nervously. 'How can a plant eat me?'

'Carnivorous plants and Land of the Giants don't forget Fluke. Everything is so much bigger and different here, you said it yourself earlier, remember?' said Tash laughing.

'It's not funny Tash,' he grumbled, desperately trying to keep calm, not move and hopefully free himself. 'I don't want to get eaten by a plant, I mean a dinosaur maybe, at least it would be a bit more heroic, but a plant? I'd be the laughing stock of the dinosaur world,' he finished by shaking his head.

'We'll get you untied Fluke, somehow, not sure how yet, but we will, I think, well possibly, just hold tight and don't go anywhere,' chuckled Tash.

'You're enjoying this, aren't you?' Fluke muttered, 'so you're all moving around OK, why haven't any of you been captured?' he asked.

Tops stepped in with the answer, 'There's only one plant, and it only has one mouth Fluke. It's captured its dinner, so we'll all be OK until it's ready for its next meal.'

Suddenly Fluke felt the vines tighten around his leg and he felt himself being dragged towards the vegetation, the thought of what was lurking behind the bush filled him with dread.

'Somebody help,' he shouted. Fluke lost his footing, slipped and was being dragged roughly over the ground. Tash grabbed one free paw, Amos the other, and they both pulled Fluke in the opposite direction.

'Oh great, so now I'm being used as a tug of war rope,' complained Fluke, 'don't let go you two, please don't let go!' he begged.

Try as they might and even with the super strength of Amos, the plant was winning. Fluke was being pulled slowly but surely towards the hidden carnivorous plant hiding behind the bushes.

Venus dogtrap...

Fluke was dragged unceremoniously through the bushes, his paws left grooves in the soil where he had attempted to stop himself, when suddenly there it was. A huge Venus flytrap, or as Fluke was thinking *a Venus dogtrap*. It was massive, so much bigger than anything they had ever seen before.

He gulped as he was dragged towards its open mouth. He looked up, then wished he hadn't as he saw two lines of what looked like sharp teeth; one set on the upper mouth with a second set lined up on the lower mouth. Fluke imagined the carnivorous plant was grinning, as it had Fluke right by the entrance to its gaping mouth.

The vines hoisted Fluke high into the air, dangling him upside down. As he hovered over the open mouth he glanced down and saw Tash grab hold of the magic suitcase. The vines released their grip and Fluke fell headfirst towards the opening. He had a soft landing on what can only be described as a huge tongue covered in soft bristles and then saw the two rows of teeth spring shut.

It went dark, but surprisingly not totally dark. Tash had sprung into action and at the last minute threw the magic case, successfully wedging it between the upper and lower sets of teeth, leaving a small gap, not big enough to crawl through, but big enough to allow some fresh air and light to shine through.

'Fluke, can you hear us? Are you OK in there?' shouted a concerned Tash, peering through the small gap that their magic case had made.

'Yeah, I'm OK. It's a bit dark in here though,' came Fluke's muffled reply.

'Whatever you do Fluke, do not, and I mean DO NOT move a muscle, stay perfectly still,' Tash breathed a huge sigh of relief that Fluke for now was OK.

'Why?' came the muffled reply from Fluke.

'It's like a Venus flytrap that dad grows in his greenhouse to capture those pesky flies in the summer. I've read about them, if you don't move for a while the plant thinks it's not food or anything edible and will open its mouth and spit you out.'

'OK, so I can't move for a little while, that's not so bad. How long have I got to wait?' Fluke asked.

Silence followed, so Fluke repeated his question.

Peter whistled and turned to look the other away. Tash and Tops found something of interest to look at in a bush and walked off. It was left to Amos to break the bad news, 'Err, about twelve hours Fluke, maybe a bit less if you're lucky.'

'*TWELVE* hours,' said a shocked Fluke, 'I can't sit still for five minutes let alone twelve hours,' he whined, the panic rising in his voice.

Captured...

Their escort of soldier ants were not happy. The Nummers were pushed, shoved and poked roughly by the angry ants as they were escorted and marched back towards the sleeping zone. The volcano was beginning to wake up, the night shift had finished, any building blocks that had been formed were cooling down, and soon it would be the turn of the day shift to help build the mighty walls.

Nat looked up with sleep filled, bleary eyes, and spied Papa and Mama being brought back to join the rest. 'So what happened last night?' he whispered once the guards had left them securely tied up. 'How far did you get?' he asked curiously, then yawned and stretched his aching muscles.

'All the way down Nat. We saw the city, the river of flowing magma...' replied Papa.

'And the building blocks. We saw how the blocks were made. These *Bigfoot* or *Sasquatch* are super intelligent Nat,' Mama continued, 'and they've got the ants, spiders and all you dinosaurs doing the hard labour.'

'So why didn't you escape?' Nat shook his large head in disbelief, 'I really thought you'd be smart and get out while you could and that we'd not see you again. Glad you're back though, it would be a bit quiet around here without you both,' he chuckled.

'We were looking for escape routes as well Nat, so when the time is right we can all get out quickly and smoothly,' said Papa, who then noticed the guards returning, forcing the long line of dinosaurs back to work. One of the ants came up to the Nummers, took hold of their restraints, fiddled around with the knots and winked.

Was it just a twitch in the ants eye or did the ant actually wink at them? Papa was about to say something to Mama when he was handed his pickaxe and Mama her shovel. *Another long hard day to look forward to* he thought, and couldn't help but glance over to the ant that had either twitched or winked and who now seemed to be smiling.

The ant then turned to face the other way and Papa soon forgot about it as he was ordered to get stuck into work, the click clicking voices of the ants spread down the line.

Meeting of the elders...

Hundreds of dinosaurs had gathered, all types were present, from the smallest to the largest. They had joined together for this large gathering, a never before seen meeting of the elders from each herd. The message sent to each herd was important and nobody wanted to miss the meeting. Each herd was represented by their most senior figure, *the dinosaur elder;* a herd leader, who was a figure to which every dinosaur, young and old, looked up to and totally respected.

Amos's dad was the leader of his particular herd. As he stepped to the top of a large mound to speak, a hush fell across the plains. Looking up he saw silent expectant faces staring back, waiting for his words of wisdom. Even the flying Pteranodons seemed to be listening as they soared gracefully through the air.

'Friends...' his voice bellowed and carried to the furthest point, 'we have a choice to make. We have a new enemy and it is now obvious that the soldier ants and spiders have been turned against us by this new tribe of creatures. We thought it was just a rumour, but our son...' he turned to his wife who had a tear streaming down her face, 'has gone on a mission to rescue his best friend Nat from the volcano. We are certain that our youngsters are being kidnapped by these hideous creatures, and we can't let it continue, we have to act now.'

'How can we be sure they've been kidnapped?' a voice from the middle of the pack shouted.

Amos's dad looked across to the *Troodon*, a two legged dinosaur which stood about two metres tall, her head barely visible amongst the throng.

'Troody, isn't it?' asked Amos's dad kindly. 'We've never met properly I know, but our herds have known each other for years. We all move from plain to plain together. You must have noticed that one by one our youngsters have gone missing? A lot of friends we all know have been affected. Well now I need for you all to meet someone who has escaped the volcano. His name is Panop,' and he stood aside to let the Panoplosaurus stand nervously on the high mound.

He was a seven metre long lizard with bulky body armour, four short stumpy legs, a short neck and long tail. The bony plates that covered his body also had short spikes on his sides and neck. He looked fearsome but was actually very shy and nervous.

Clearing his voice, he started to speak. 'It's true, I too was kidnapped, forced into work but was fortunate to escape one evening. The creatures in charge use the ants and spiders to guard the slaves who are helping to build an underground city with huge walls to make it a fortress. There are loads of dinosaurs in the volcano being used as slaves,' he looked to Amos's dad, who nodded allowing Panop to step back.

Murmurings of conversation rippled through the ranks as this new information was digested.

The mother of Amos's friend stepped to the front, turned around to speak to the crowd. 'Our Nat has been missing for ages,' she confirmed, 'he just disappeared one day whilst playing. He must have got too close to the volcano and has not been seen since. We must join together and try to find our missing family and friends.'

Amos's dad hushed the expectant crowd. 'Two adults from each herd will accompany myself, we'll leave the plains this afternoon and head for the volcano.'

It was time for action and last minute plans were made. They would leave as soon as they could. Amos's dad and Nat's mum stood shoulder-to-shoulder, staring towards the volcano. 'We'll get Nat back I promise, and knowing the trouble my son Amos gets into, we'll probably need to rescue him as well,' he chuckled.

Get me out of here...

How long have I been in here? Fluke thought to himself, wishing he had a watch to check, although as dark as it was inside he probably wouldn't be able to see the time anyway. He felt a sneeze brewing deep down, so he carefully pinched his nose and held his breath until the feeling went away, because when Fluke sneezed it was always a humdinger! Not moving a muscle for twelve hours? Did they not know how hard it was to stay perfectly still for that length of time?

He'd tried sleeping but gave that idea up as he was fearful he'd start sleep walking again. Last time he did that was in Ancient Greece and look what trouble he'd gotten himself into then!

'How you doing Fluke?' Tash's concerned voice could be heard from outside, interrupting Fluke's thoughts. 'Hang on in there, not long to go now,' she said.

'Oh everything's just rosy Tash, you should try it sometime!' said Fluke sarcastically, 'this must be in the top ten attractions on any holiday list,' he continued.

'Just think, we'll be laughing about this later,' said Tash.

'Probably,' agreed Fluke brightening up, feeling confident his ordeal was nearly over. 'Do you think I might get in the Guinness World Records book for staying still the longest in a Venus dogtrap?'

Tash chuckled, 'it might be worthwhile looking into Fluke,' when all of a sudden, something started to happen.

'I can see more light Tash,' said an excited Fluke, as the gap between the two jaws parted slightly.

'Get ready Fluke,' whispered Amos.

The mighty jaws suddenly sprang open causing everybody to stagger back in surprise and watch in awe as Fluke was literally spat from the mouth.

'Yipee! Get me out of hereeeeeeee!' Fluke shouted gleefully as he hurtled through the air, eventually landing on his backside in the middle of a prickly bush.

'Everybody run before the vines start looking for more food,' Amos said and broke into a fast jog. Everybody began to follow, except Fluke who was limping behind.

'Keep up,' urged Tash looking over her shoulder at Fluke trailing behind.

'I've got cramp and my leg muscles have stiffened up...' whined Fluke, 'not moving a muscle for twelve hours is harder than it looks,' he continued, but the thought of being caught by any stray vines spurred him on, and soon he was overtaking Tash in the dash to escape the Venus dogtrap.

You can't swim in that...

Amos had been leading from the front so when Fluke whizzed past he began to slow and let the rest catch up. 'Fluke, you can slow down now, I think we're safely clear from any more creeping vines,' he laughed and watched as first Tash, then Peter and Tops all caught up.

They had stopped at the edge of a very large area of swampland. Dark brown bubbling liquid lay ahead with various sized stepping stone islands dotted here and there. The width of swamp was huge, with no obvious direct way around, so the only option they had was attempt to cross at its narrowest point.

Fluke was bent over double, paws resting on his legs as he tried to get his breath back. 'Crikey that was close, when we get home Tash...' he gasped, 'remind me not to go anywhere near the Venus flytrap in dad's greenhouse,' and then he flopped on the floor, panting.

Tash joined him and they settled down for a few minutes break. Looking ahead she let her eyes rove over the horrid looking and foul smelling liquid. 'So Amos, I just want to be sure there's nothing in the swamp that wants to eat us, is there?' Silence followed, so Tash said warily, 'Amos?'

Amos shrugged and looked at Tops, 'shall you tell them or shall I?'

Tops spoke up, 'well, it's only a rumour, but the wise dinosaur elders say the swamps are home to eight legged creatures that swim below the surface waiting to catch anything silly enough to cross. But it is only a rumour though and probably, well possibly, almost certainly not true. Maybe!'

Fluke shook his head, 'if you think I'm swimming in that...' and pointed his paw towards the swamp...'

'You can't swim in that Fluke,' said Tash, 'walk across the stepping stones maybe, sail across for sure, but no swimming.'

'Either way we have to cross it though. There's no short cut I suppose?' he turned and looked hopefully at Amos, who shook his head, 'didn't think so,' sighed Fluke.

They gathered around to discuss the best option. It was agreed they would hop and jump from one small island to the next. It was pointed out by Amos, who once again confirmed it was just a rumour that the wise old dinosaur elders had said, that there was a maze of islands and only one way through the maze. If you hopped onto the wrong island at any point, by the time you got to the far side of the swamp, the gap to jump onto dry land was too vast, so you'd have to go back to the beginning to start again. That's if you could find your way back, as it was rumoured some dinosaurs attempting the crossing had been left stranded for months out in the vast swamplands and were never seen again.

'So if these dinosaur elders are so wise, why hasn't anybody actually drawn a map across?' asked Tash, scratching an itchy spot behind her ear.

Several more minutes passed as they stood on firm ground. In front of them were a dozen or so small islands, each one easily in reach, it was just a case of choosing which one to jump on to start their crossing.

'You first!' giggled Tash, pushing Fluke in the back, causing him to stumble and nearly fall in.

'No, I think Amos should have the honour of being the first to go,' replied Fluke, stepping back and waving Amos forward.

One small jump at a time...

*A*mos took the first hesitant leap to lead the way, closely followed by Tops then Peter, with Fluke and Tash bringing up the rear. The islands were within easy reach of each other and became ever so crowded once everybody was safely on. Although some of the islands were slightly larger and had trees growing on them, most were just plain old empty sandbanks.

Now, as this was a Fluke and Tash adventure, things would eventually start to go wrong and they didn't have to wait too long for the problems to start. Taking it in turns to choose which island was next, they had safely navigated about thirty islands when they all landed safely on the latest; one of the larger islands, with huge water lilies floating around the edge. They walked to the furthest point and stood staring ahead. The gap to the next island was huge, the leap was way too much, even for an Olympic long jump champion.

'Now what do we do?' asked Peter.

'Well, you could probably fly across Peter if you'd only learnt how to flap your wings properly!' said Tops.

'We'll have to go back one stage and take a different route,' confirmed Amos, who turned around to walk back to the other side of the island.

Gazing back the way they'd come from, it was now obvious they weren't exactly sure which island they had last been on, as there were so many to choose from.

'I think it was the middle one, that one over there,' said Tops pointing.

'No it wasn't that one,' said Peter confidently, 'it was the one next to it, I'm sure it was,' he continued and flapped his wings in the general direction.

'You're all wrong,' said Fluke pushing his way to the front. 'I bet you it was the third one along,' he said, but then his voice waivered slightly, 'well, I think it was that one anyway! I can see why they call it a maze, all I can see are islands dotted here and there but now looking at them I haven't the foggiest idea which route we took!' said Fluke in alarm.

'Now this could be a problem,' said Tash, 'if we pick the wrong island we're never going to get back and we'll probably end up going round in circles.'

'I don't fancy being stuck out here,' said Fluke, who had picked up a long stick and dipped into the thick brown gloop that made up the swamp to try and see how deep it was. The stick slipped from his paw and started to float on the surface, a grin spread over his face, 'I've just had an idea and for once it might actually work...' he said.

A friend in the camp...

The work party was in full swing. The Nummers were digging and shovelling; sacks were being filled at a great speed, and dinosaurs carried the lava rocks off to be crushed and dispersed onto the ground outside the volcano.

'Is it me or is that ant over there smiling at us?' whispered Papa.

Mama turned her head slightly to see which one her husband was talking about. 'I think he is you know, and he was also the one that tied us back up after we had been recaptured. Do you think these knots are looser than they first were?' Mama asked, 'because I don't think he's tied them up properly.'

Papa tested his own knot and found with satisfaction that Mama was right, the knots were loose. 'He also winked at me earlier on,' said Papa.

'Winked? Are you sure? Maybe he had a bit of dust in his eye,' said Mama.

'Let's keep an eye on him to see what he does next,' suggested Papa and saw Nat returning with empty sacks waiting for more lava rocks.

The long day finally came to an end. A dinner of vegetable stew was served and devoured by the hungry workers and then it was time for a well-earned night's sleep. All was quiet in the camp when Papa, who slept with one eye open, heard a shuffling noise getting closer. He quickly closed his eye, pretending he was fast asleep, when the shuffling noise halted directly in front of where Papa and Mama had laid down to rest.

A voice, and not the click clicking of the ants, broke the silence. 'It's me, the winking ant. I'm a friend, here to help and not the enemy like those others,' and then what was said next really surprised Papa, 'I'm here to help you all try and escape...'

Boat building...

'It's easy Tash, come on, we can at least try,' begged Fluke, 'what have we got to lose?' he said.

Tash thought long and hard, 'so what makes you think we can build a boat?' she asked.

'Have you forgotten already Tash?' teased Fluke, 'we've only just recently met one of the best boat builders in the world. I can't believe you've already forgotten about our Egyptian adventure with that lovely cruise down the Nile.'

'Of course,' Tash slapped her paw against her head, 'Paneferher, master boat builder of Egypt, how could I be so forgetful. Have we got the right equipment?'

'Ta-da!' said Fluke, triumphantly pointing to a large bush of reeds growing nearby, 'we'll build our very own Felucca in no time, what more could we possibly need?' he asked.

'Apart from skill and twenty years' boat building experience,' said Tash, chuckling, 'but like you say, what have we got to lose!'

Amos, Tops and Peter helped gather big bundles of reeds and looked on in wonderment as the boats slowly began to take shape.

Night was drawing in by the time they had finished building. They had constructed two large reed bed boats, similar in design to the boats that were built in Ancient Egypt. They had tied two boats together, side-by-side, as Amos and Tops were a bit large and Fluke figured one boat wouldn't be big enough to hold everybody.

Tash stood back to admire their handiwork. 'Well, they might not be exactly the same as the grand sailing boats that sail up and down the River Nile, but they're sort of boat shaped I guess, so now we'll have to see whether they actually float!' With Fluke's assistance she dragged the two boats tethered together to the edge of the swamp and there they sat, bobbing low in the grungy brown, gloopy swamp, but amazingly they actually floated.

Lurking deep down...

large, single, beady eye broke the surface of the swamp and swivelled around 360 degrees, finally coming to rest on a group of figures stood on the edge of the large sand bank island. It had felt the vibrations coursing below the surface of the swamp when they had jumped from island to island, but now they were stranded. It practically rubbed its eight tentacles together under the surface in anticipation of a nice dinner.

It counted five creatures. Two of them it completely disregarded as they were too big and would take a lot of handling, plus it didn't feel *that* hungry. A third looked too skinny and had thin flapping wings that would just get in the way, and it was hardly worth the effort. The fourth and fifth looked promising, and were currently dragging a lot of reeds tied together to the shoreline. A boat maybe? It was sort of boat shaped and it did actually float, but not for much longer, the creature chuckled to itself. The spotty one looked tasty but so did the other small furry one, both looked just about the right size.

The eye disappeared back below the surface. It didn't like bright light and preferred the gloom of the swamp. It would wait a bit longer until they had left the safety of the shore and were floating along on their homemade boat. It also happened to like reeds, so eating them *and* the reed boat wouldn't be a problem.

HMS Swamp Dodger...

'Shouldn't we have a ceremony before we launch the boat Fluke?' asked Tash proudly, who then proceeded to inspect their new vessel, checking for any sign of leaks, 'I mean we have to name her before her maiden voyage,' she continued, 'and it's good luck as well.'

'How about *HMS Swamp Dodger*?' Said Fluke chuckling. It was agreed they would name the boat and officially launch it into the swamp before they set they're paws aboard their new vessels.

Amos and Tops, being rather large, had to straddle the two boats. One set of feet in one boat and the other set of feet in the other. The boat began to sink slightly but soon righted itself and bobbed merrily in the grungy brown swamp awaiting its final occupants. Peter was next aboard *HMS Swamp Dodger* and finally Fluke sat in the rear of the left-hand boat, whilst Tash sat at the back of the right-hand boat.

Fluke had located two long sticks which would act as the oars to help move the craft in the right direction and steer it around any island sandbanks. Passing one to Tash they cast off and straight away the boat started to wobble.

'Whoa!' exclaimed Fluke hanging onto the sides as the rocking motion threatened to spill them overboard. 'Stand still Amos and don't move a muscle, you're rocking the boat!'

'How long for?' asked Amos without turning around, standing stock-still.

'About twelve hours,' chuckled Fluke.

'Oh funny Fluke, you're so funny,' said Amos.

Fluke started to sing some sea shanty songs, causing Tash to laugh.

'Listen to him! He thinks he's a proper old sea dog now, next he'll be getting a wooden leg, patch over his eye and a parrot sat on his shoulder and calling everybody "*matey*" and saying "*shiver me timbers,*" chuckled Tash.

Fluke laughed and poked his oar at Tash, 'you're just jealous of my wonderful singing voice,' and carried on paddling.

Tash was sat on their magic case which had been stowed carefully in the bottom of the boat and began to rummage in her satchel. Finding the torch, she passed it to Peter, who was stood at the front.

'Shine this ahead of us Peter, so we can see where to steer, it's getting dark and we need to get to the other side as fast as we can.'

It was almost as if somebody had turned off the light switch, such was the speed of the approaching night. The torch thankfully shone brightly, leading the way as *HMS Swamp Dodger* was being navigated between the islands, heading, they hoped, for the safety of dry land far off in the distance.

Amos, who was stood tall in the boat, followed the light beam, guiding them around sandbanks when necessary, so was the first to see ripples in the water fast approaching their boat. 'Err, not sure what it is, but somethings heading towards us, and it's heading this way rapidly,' he said, trying to adjust his eyes in the dark.

Fluke stopped his rowing and moved toward the front. Reaching over to the other boat, he took the torch off Peter and shone it around the swamp, but failed to see anything.

'I saw something Fluke, right over there, heading this way,' said Amos.

It was then that Fluke spotted a long line of bubbles rising to the surface right in front of the boat. Following the line of bubbles with the torch beam, he watched in wonderment as the bubbles promptly disappeared under their boat.

Something had submerged and was swimming underneath, and whatever it was it was big. So big in fact they felt the boat move and partially lift out of the water, causing Fluke to drop his torch into the bottom of the boat.

A cry of alarm was heard from the rear. Everyone at the front turned around and were greeted with a horrific sight.

Long tentacles had snaked their way into the boat and were thrashing around. A startled Tash tried in vain to get out of the way, but one of the tentacles found her and began to wrap itself around a leg and hoist her aloft. Grabbing hold of the first thing she could lay her paws on, she held firmly onto their magic case.

Tash was lifted and suspended in the air, and just as she shouted out a warning the creature dragged her and the magic case overboard. There was a loud splash, followed by a stunned silence.

Saving captain Tash...

The silence only lasted for seconds before Fluke and Peter leapt into action. Fluke, although he couldn't swim, didn't care. His best friend was in serious trouble. Not thinking about the consequences he dived overboard, armed with nothing more than the long oar, and was closely followed by Peter who stood on the edge of the boat, clutching the torch that Fluke had dropped seconds ago, and dived in.

In a strange way Fluke was glad the swamp monster was so big and huge, as he didn't have too many problems locating the beast. It was dark and gloomy down under the swamp, but thankfully in an instant he located Tash. Holding his breath he struggled to free his best friend from the tentacle, aware that at any minute he too may get caught. He used the oar and gave the beast a thump on its head, repeating the exercise again and again until he noticed the tentacle begin to loosen its hold.

Peter had joined the fray alongside Fluke, and with his long sharp beak he pecked at the monster's tentacle. The torch was still turned on and shone brightly into the eyes of the beast.

The swamp monster wasn't used to this, most of his victims just gave up. It didn't know what to do, but with the constant banging on its head, the sharp pecks to its tentacle and now the bright light shining into its eyes, which it hated, it decided it had had enough and released the small furry creature, deciding instead to sensibly wait a bit longer and pick an easier target.

You steer and I'll drive...

Amos and Tops looked over the edge of the boat into the dark swamp not knowing what they could do to help. It was then that three heads broke the surface right next to the rear of the boat and began to clamber back over the edge.

Tash followed Fluke and Peter and stood in the stern of the boat, all three dripping wet with brown swampy slime gunk. Looking back over the edge Tash saw their magic case floating on the surface and leant over to retrieve it. Holding the handle, she began to drag it back to the boat. Still floating in the swamp it suddenly sprang into life and started making rumbling noises, coughed and spluttered into life, churning up a froth of disgusting brown liquid behind them. Their boat started to pick up speed, as the magic case propelled them through the swamp.

'Quick Fluke, grab hold of the oars, you steer and I'll drive,' shouted Tash gleefully, hanging onto the handle over her shoulder, 'the case has started working again!'

Not only had the case sprung to life, but it was proving very useful as an outboard motor. *HMS*

Swamp Dodger had transformed itself from a row boat into a speedboat, and sped off. Peter stood at the bow and shone the torch, which although had taken a soaking was thankfully still working. A beacon of light shone brightly, allowing Fluke to navigate a path successfully through and between the islands, leaving the swamp monster far behind.

Land was spotted by Amos and realising they were all now safe, the crew of *HMS Swamp Dodger* breathed a huge sigh of relief.

'Thank you for your help. I can't believe how quickly it all happened, I really didn't know what to do,' said Tash. 'And as for you...' she pointed a paw towards Fluke, 'I'm getting you a beginners swimming certificate when we get home! Fluke, you actually swam!' she laughed, 'I know how much you hate water, so to dive in like that was amazingly brave.'

Dry land at last...

They leapt back onto firm dry land and stood watching. Their boat, not designed for such speed, began to break up. It was a sad moment, but they all stood around and watched as *HMS Swamp Dodger* slipped slowly below the surface, thankful it had helped save them.

Dawn was fast approaching, nobody had slept, but they were still buzzing from their lucky escape so nobody cared or noticed how tired they actually were.

'It was almost as if our case knew we were in trouble and came to our aid,' said Fluke, patting the worn brown exterior with affection.

'True, very true Fluke. I'm also glad it's started working again, as I think we may have more use for it pretty soon,' said Tash.

Tash tipped the contents of her satchel onto the ground, grabbed the map and laid it on the ground, carefully spreading out the creases. She studied the map carefully and said 'So to get back on track we've got to walk across these open plains,' she pointed to the light brown area on the map, and when they all agreed she began to stow the items back inside her satchel, the map last to go in and within easy reach.

The group readied themselves. Tash led from the front and began the long walk across the open grassland, with Fluke bringing up the rear and carrying the case.

Dino spotting...

At first the open plains seemed void of any life, but the further they went, and with the smoking volcano looming closer, they started to see a variety of creatures all criss-crossing the open expanse laid out in front of them.

Fluke was beside himself with excitement when he started spotting herds of dinosaurs. Rummaging in his own satchel he took out a 'Dino Spotters Handbook' and leafed through some pages until he got to the section labelled *Late Cretaceous Period* and pointed excitedly with his paw, 'over there, a herd of *Ankylosaurus*, large armour-plated creatures with huge clubs for their tails,' and pointed again, 'Ooh, ooh, look over there! A pair of *Gorgosaurus* and it looks like they're chasing something!' This carried on for several minutes, with Fluke spotting *Troodons, Diceratops, Bugenasaura,* until a shiver went down his spine. He stopped in his tracks and told everybody to lay low.

After they had laid flat on the ground, well as flat to the ground as Amos and Tops could manage, Tash whispered, 'what's the matter Fluke? What have you spotted?'

Raising his binoculars to his eyes he swung the lenses around, tried to focus them and whispered back, 'there on the horizon are a pair of *Tyrannosaurus Rex*, and they're heading this way.'

This piece of news sent shivers down all their spines except Tash, who boldly stood up, retrieved the magic case from Fluke and promptly said, 'well, come on then, since we're here we best get a closer look.'

'Are you mad?' whispered Fluke, pointing, 'it's a *Tyrannosaurus*,' as if that alone was enough reason to start fleeing in the opposite direction. 'If he spots us we're in big trouble,' and carried on spying the far off predator with his binoculars.

'Look, you've nearly been eaten by a Venus Flytrap, I've nearly come a cropper to an eight legged swamp monster, the least we can do is get a closer look at the King of Dinosaurs,' and she set about adjusting the controls on their case and hopped aboard, 'besides, if they're heading this way we better divert their attention and steer them away in a different direction.'

Fluke looked at her, shook his head in bewilderment, laughed and said 'OK, you win. Let's go and have a game of chase with a T-Rex!' and sat behind Tash on the case.

Turning her head, Tash turned to Amos, Tops and Peter and said, 'you three better wait here, we're going to investigate and we'll be back shortly!' and with that the case hovered several feet off the ground and shot off like a rocket, heading directly towards danger.

'Feels good, doesn't it Fluke, to have the case working again,' shouted Tash above the noise of the wind, as they skimmed a few feet above the ground.

'Let's just hope it stays working then Tash, because if it fails when we're buzzing around them...' he pointed to the two fast approaching Tyrannosaurus, 'then one of us will be in all sorts of trouble.'

'One of us will be in trouble?' queried Tash, turning her head.

'OK, you'll be in trouble Tash, because like I said back home, I plan to run faster than you!'

Tyrannosaurus v Triceratops...

'*Y*ee ha!' shouted Fluke and Tash together, as they joined in with the herds of dinosaurs criss-crossing their paths that Fluke had spotted moments ago. Tash manoeuvred the case and adjusted the speed so they were flying directly alongside a herd of *Bugenasaura,* who ran on two legs and were pretty swift.

'Look at the wonderful green colours of their scaly skin,' said Fluke, as they passed slowly, and one dinosaur glanced over to see what had overtaken it, its large yellow eye fixed on Fluke, causing him to shiver. On the opposite side was a pack of fleeing *Troodons* who had spotted the two Tyrannosaurus and were making a quick getaway.

'They've got the right idea Tash,' muttered Fluke.

'What do you mean?' asked Tash.

'Everything is running away from the two T-Rex, either crossing our path or heading towards us, and we're the only ones daft enough to head directly toward them.'

'Not the only ones Fluke, look!' she said and pointed ahead. 'Now this could be interesting,' said Tash, 'looks like four dinosaurs have challenged the two Tyrannosaurus. They're standing their ground and won't budge,' she began to slow the case down.

Fluke looked over Tash's shoulder at the scene and gasped, 'a small herd of Triceratops. You don't think they might be related to Tops do you?' asked a concerned Fluke, hoping his friend wasn't watching the show with Amos.

Tash began to carefully circle the two sets of dinosaurs. One of the T-Rex charged the Triceratopses but backed off at the last minute. The second Tyrannosaurus gave out an earth-shattering roar that seemed to shake the ground, but still the Triceratopses showed no fear and bellowed back almost as loudly. The lead Triceratops turned to face its potential attacker, pawed the ground with one if its hooves and made a dummy charge, which actually forced the T-Rex to step back.

The two sets of dinosaurs were evenly matched. The Tyrannosaurus had better eyesight, were faster in a straight line and had an incredibly strong bite with an impressive set of sharp teeth that could crush almost anything.

The Triceratops however, were smaller and could move a lot quicker in different directions.

They also had an impressive neck frill, which measured a metre across and was made entirely of strong bone, ideal for protecting their neck and head from bite marks. But their most impressive feature, and one that the Tyrannosaurus were very wary of, were the three sharp horns used to defend themselves from attack.

One false move from either creature could end in disaster, so both dinosaurs were being extra cautious. One of the T-Rex charged again but got a prod from one of the sharp horns, which must have hurt because the Tyrannosaurus yelped and backed off.

Both sets of gladiators eyed each other warily and it looked like a draw was a fair result as they slowly backed away from each other. The Triceratopses went one way and unfortunately for Fluke and Tash the two Tyrannosaurus started to head towards Amos, Tops and Peter.

Game of chase...

The two Tyrannosaurus lumbered off, heading directly towards Tash and Fluke's friends, and with their excellent eyesight and keen sense of smell it wouldn't take them too long to spot the three young quivering dinosaurs.

'We've got to get them to change direction Fluke,' said Tash, the worry in her voice clearly showing.

'Get in front of the lead T-Rex and see if it chases us,' suggested Fluke.

Tash sped up, got in front, and then slowed down a bit and started to zig-zag, changing course to see if they were followed. Fluke looked over his shoulder and gulped nervously as one of the Tyrannosaurus instantly spotted them and gave chase. It opened its huge mouth, each jaw brimming with sharp teeth, and let out an ear-splitting roar which made both Fluke and Tash's fur stand on end.

Tash looked over her shoulder checking to see if her evasive tactics were working, she started to laugh as this game of chase was easier than she first thought.

Turning back to the front she suddenly stopped laughing. Fluke also turned around to face the front, now fully satisfied they were at a safe distance, when he too stopped laughing, the smile immediately wiped off his face as well. Directly in front of them, jaws wide open, was the second T-Rex. He must have peeled away and taken a different direction. All the zig-zagging and weaving that Tash had done to confuse the first T-Rex had steered them into the path of the second beast.

At the very last second they flew straight through its open mouth, both Fluke and Tash felt its hot breath on their backs, as they managed to avoid the sharp teeth and jaws as they snapped shut on thin air.

'Can I open my eyes now Tash?' asked Fluke, 'I know we wanted to get a closer look but that was a bit too close for my liking,' he joked and turned around to watch the two Tyrannosaurus run into each other, which started a squabble between the two.

Tash sped off in the opposite direction leading the pair of T-Rex away from Amos, Tops and Peter, gradually increasing the gap between them and the two chasing beasts. Satisfied they were now out of danger, she turned the case in a long arc, and headed back to safety to meet up with their nervous friends, who were trying unsuccessfully to blend into the background.

Amos was hiding his large body behind a small thin tree, Peter was hiding behind Amos, and Tops was equally unsuccessful in trying to disguise himself by hiding behind a small rock.

'Will you look at those three trying to hide!' whispered Tash to Fluke, and then said in a loud voice, 'Where's Amos, Tops and Peter?' chuckled Tash, 'I'm sure we left them here, I told them to wait for us.'

'I don't know Tash, they were here a few minutes ago, where could they possibly have gone?' joked Fluke.

'Pssst, we're over here!' whispered Amos.

'Who said that?' asked Fluke, pretending to look all round. 'Tash, the trees and rocks are talking to us!' he replied, desperately trying to keep a straight face and not laugh.

'No, seriously it's us; Amos, Tops and Peter!' whispered Tops, 'Is it safe to come out yet?' he asked.

'Oh, they're you are, the masters of disguise. We couldn't see a thing, could we Tash?' said Fluke and the pair couldn't contain themselves any longer as they burst out laughing, rolling around on the floor with a fit of the giggles.

Isn't *Bigfoot* just a myth...?

They left the plains unscathed, relieved to have escaped the clutches of the two hungry Tyrannosaurus. They walked for another hour, constantly looking up at the large smouldering volcano that was getting closer and closer with each step they took, now realising exactly how huge it was.

Plans were made and discussions were had about various ways of getting access into the volcano undetected. The only known way, according to the dinosaur elders, was crossing a rocky path or type of footbridge that led right into some caves and then into the volcano but it would surely be well guarded, and guarded by what or whom?

They were so close now they could almost reach out and touch the volcanic rock and feel the heat being generated, as this was for sure an active volcano. Seeing it from a distance and hearing the rumours was one thing, but making camp at the base of the volcano was another.

A small camp was made right by the edge of the lake, the bright midday sun shining brightly on its surface. Fluke and Tash crept off to find the main entrance, came upon the rocky path that allowed you access and discovered it was guarded by soldier ants. And not your average soldier ant either, but whopping great big ants with sharp looking spears. They hid behind some bushes and watched the comings and goings.

'Would you see the size of those ants,' exclaimed Fluke, 'dad would have to get a huge pot of ant powder at home to get rid of those pesky creatures,' he chuckled and then gasped, as out strode two hairy creatures.

'Are they what I think they are...?' Fluke's voice trailed off as they spied the newcomers issuing orders to the ant security guards.

'*Bigfoot or Sasquatch...*' Tash's voice also trailed off in wonderment, 'People and scientists always thought they were just a myth, a hoax spun by the locals to encourage tourism, but there they are. Maybe our scientists don't know as much as they think they do Fluke,' said Tash.

They watched a while longer, keen to see if there was any way they could distract the guards, but for now it seemed likely they couldn't get access through the front. They hoped that there would be another way inside. Creeping silently back to camp they reported their findings.

It was agreed they'd rest up a while and think things through, no point in rushing headlong into danger. They had come this far and waited a couple of days, so a bit longer wouldn't make much difference.

The big blue lake...

Fluke used his satchel as a pillow and dozed off. Tash lay back on the grassy bank deep in thought, but soon fell asleep too. Amos and Tops wandered off into the bushes trying to find something tasty to eat, which left Peter wide awake and hungry.

The lake was a pale, light blue, so clean without any pollution, it was almost crystal clear. You could see the lake bottom sloping away, getting deeper and deeper the further out you waded. He paddled out into the lake as far as he dared until he was waist deep and stood on a rocky ledge. One more step and he would walk off the edge and plunge into some seriously deep water. He stuck his head under and shuddered as it was cold. Looking all around, he hoped to spot some fish that might be easy to catch. No luck though, as they were all swimming just a few feet out of reach, as if teasing him to take one more step that could prove costly.

Peter's eyesight was superb, and the water was so clear he could see far off into the distance. Just before he ran out of breath he saw a canyon, a huge underwater trench snaking its way along the lake bed, winding its way on the lake floor like a path that led right up to the base of the volcano.

He removed his head, shook droplets of water from his face, took a big deep breath and plunged underwater again. Huge underwater ferns and plants as big as trees grew wildly on the sides of the trench, providing loads of hidey holes for creatures of all sizes. He stared at a dark patch, an entrance to an underwater cave possibly?

His hunger was forgotten as he started to think that maybe they could somehow sneak into the volcano through this underwater cave. But how, as they couldn't hold their breath for any longer than a minute, and what if it wasn't an entrance after all? He felt giddy with so many thoughts rushing through his head and lack of oxygen due to holding his breath too long, so he re-surfaced for more air and to give him time to think things through.

The friendly ant...

It was late afternoon. The work party was winding down and were enjoying a short rest. The soldier ants allowed the workers to have a break, they seemed to perform much better after some rest.

Mama was sat next to Nat, Papa and Dice the Diceratops. Two soldier ants came over, stood looking down at the group resting and began a conversation that consisted of a series of click, clicking noises which came from their mouths. A spear was used to prod them all to a standing position.

'Hey, what's that for and what have we done?' complained Dice, clearly upset that their rest break appeared to have come to an abrupt end. 'We've not finished our break yet, why are you picking on us?'

Papa was closely watching one of the ants. It was the same one that had winked at them, he was certain. 'It's OK Dice, don't get upset, if they think break's over then it must be.'

'But it's not fair...' Dice started to complain loudly but never got to finish his sentence, as Papa pulled him away before he could cause a scene.

'Leave it Dice,' Papa whispered, 'I think I know what's going on,' and he tried to cover Dice's mouth before he could say anything. 'You're just going to have to trust me on this...'

Submarine...

'You have got to be kidding me...' exclaimed Fluke, still half asleep and bleary eyed after his afternoon snooze. Thinking he had misheard, he looked at Tash, 'A submarine? How are we going to build a submarine?'

They had both been rudely awoken by an excited Peter, who stood looking down on the sleeping pair, dripping water all over them. He then proceeded to tell everybody about the underwater cave he'd discovered.

Tash took on board what she was being told and instantly came up with an idea, a crazy idea, but one which might just work. The shoreline was scattered with huge conch shells; extremely large sea shells that must have at one time or another been home to some rather large aquatic snails, their previous owners long abandoning their home.

Tash padded over to one of the large shells, laying discarded and empty on its side, which stood over six feet tall. She beckoned to Fluke who picked himself up off the floor and walked over.

'Look how big it is,' said Tash, walking around the outside and promptly disappearing. Fluke could hear her muffled voice coming from within and heard her knocking on the shell wall from the inside. He decided to follow her around the opposite side and found a large aperture, the hole that the aquatic snail would have used to retract into when resting.

Fluke found he could walk inside, not having to duck as it was so high, and he entered into an open area that looked impressively big.

Fluke's voice echoed when he spoke. 'OK, so we're in a snail shell, a very large snail shell I agree, but how is this going to help us get into the volcano?'

'I've seen experiments on the television Fluke,' replied Tash, 'if you turn a cup upside down and hold it underwater the top half of the cup has an air pocket, the trapped air inside keeps the water out.'

Fluke pondered this and it suddenly dawned on him what Tash was suggesting. 'Are you sure this will work?' he asked dubiously, 'so let me fully understand. We climb into the shell and walk along the bottom of the lake, all the while breathing in the air trapped in the shell?'

'Yep, that's about right,' nodded Tash.

How do you steer it...?

Tash opened the lid and rummaged in their magic suitcase, and with a triumphant shout located their swimming goggles they last used in Ancient Greece when they came up against Medusa. She passed a set to Fluke who adjusted the strap and fitted them snuggly over his head.

Tash sneaked up behind him, took a hold of the elastic strap holding the goggles in place, stretched it and then let go. She fell about laughing as the elastic snapped back and slapped Fluke on the back of the head.

'Ouch!' he said,' what was that for?' he turned and asked whilst rubbing the back of his head.

'Just checking they're tight enough Fluke,' laughed Tash, 'you have to be careful, can't have them slipping off whilst we're underwater,' she chuckled.

Amos and Tops righted the gigantic conch shell so it stood upright.

Tash turned to their three friends, 'You three better stay here. We may be a while, as we don't know what's waiting for us inside,' and she pointed with her paw to the waiting volcano.

Fluke disappeared inside the upturned shell and was closely followed by Tash.

'I'll drive,' said Fluke, taking his place towards what he thought was the front of the shell, 'but where's the steering wheel!' he joked.

Thankfully, even though the shell was large, it was very lightweight and they managed to hoist the shell up in the air. Holding on to the edge they walked the shell down to the water line. Amos, Tops and Peter watched in fascination as the conch shell all but waddled towards the lake edge. All they could see were two pairs of feet sticking out below the shell.

Fluke was the first to enter the water and shuddered as the temperature made him gasp.

Tash was close behind and muttered, 'crikey it's cold! My paws are freezing.' The pair of sub-mariners continued their walk on the lake bottom and with each step they got further away from the shoreline.

Amos, Tops and Peter watched as the conch shell slowly disappeared from sight and sunk below the lake surface.

Inside the shell, the water level began to rise until it was waist high. Fluke slowed his walking and turned around, 'just want to check that the water won't get any higher because of the air pocket we've got inside the shell with us?'

'Yep, it shouldn't get any higher,' confirmed Tash.

'So why are we wearing goggles then?' said Fluke.

'Oh, didn't I tell you?' said Tash

'Tell me what?' asked Fluke suspiciously, sensing Tash had maybe not told him the complete truth.

'Well, as you can see we don't have any windscreen to look out of, so we're sort of steering blind,' she said, 'and I was rather hoping that every now and then you could pop your head under the edge of the shell to see that we're heading in the right direction,' she confirmed.

'Oh were you now. I did wonder how we would steer it. Well I suppose one of us had better have a look, so here goes,' and much to Tash's surprise he took a deep breath, pinched his nose and ducked under the edge of the shell.

He looked around at the awe inspiring scene that surrounded them. His goggles thankfully stayed firmly attached. They were walking the shell in a deep gully with sloping sides that closely resembled an underwater forest with all types of underwater ferns growing wildly.

Fluke spotted the entrance to the cave and made some minor adjustments to the way the shell was pointed, and then he noticed two sets of paws standing still under the shell. He was feeling full of mischief and looked around for something he could use.

There, lying on the bottom, was an empty oyster shell, the two halves partially open. Grabbing hold, he found to his delight it still opened and shut with ease. Reaching down he clamped the shell onto Tash's paws and heard a yell of surprise come from within the shell as she began hopping from one paw to another. Chuckling to himself he bobbed back inside the conch shell and pretended nothing had happened.

'Something bit me,' wailed Tash and reached down to remove the oyster shell from her paw.

'You should be more careful where you're walking Tash,' giggled Fluke, 'anyway, at least now we're pointing in the right direction, so c'mon, the cave entrance is that way...' he pointed straight ahead, 'let's get this submarine going, full steam ahead!' and they started off again, the entrance to the volcano getting closer by the second.

We made it...

Several minutes of zig-zagging underwater, stumbling on lumps of coral, and treading on the occasional startled Flatfish, Fluke and Tash eventually made it safely through the cave entrance. Resting for a few seconds first, they both held their breath, ducked below the edge of the shell and swam to the surface.

Their two heads popped up through the surface of a large rock pool within a chamber. Looking around they spotted a rocky ledge and swam towards it. Tash was the first to spring from the water, then reached down to help hoist Fluke out. They both stood in their new surroundings unsure what to do first.

'Well, we made it Tash,' confirmed Fluke looking all around, removing his googles and resting them on top of his head. 'Part one of *"Operation Nummer"* is successfully completed.'

'Operation Nummer?' chuckled Tash looking at Fluke.

'All these secret operations on T.V. get given names, so why not ours!' he joked.

'OK, so which path do we take?' said Tash, looking at a choice of four tunnels to choose from.

'Let's play *spin the rock*,' said Fluke and reached down to grab hold of a long knobbly piece of rock and spun it on the ground. Both Fluke and Tash looked on as the stick-shaped rock slowed down and pointed to one of the middle tunnels. 'That's the one I'd have chosen anyway,' shrugged Fluke and they both headed off into the unknown.

The rocky path they were following took them on a tour of the inner volcano. Tash felt the path they were taking was spiralling slightly upwards and around every turn there were small rock pools, similar, but much smaller than the one they had used to enter the volcano.

Fluke stopped to look down into one of these pools and asked 'do you think all these rock pools are joined up outside?'

'I think so Fluke. It seems like the volcano has a lot of hidden underground entrances, these rock pools feed back into the large lake outside,' replied Tash.

They carried onwards, desperate to find the Nummers. Rounding another bend, Fluke was the first to spot two soldier ants. They were leaning up against the rock walls, backs turned and in deep conversation.

Fluke turned to Tash and raised a paw to his lips, urging Tash to be quiet. 'You take the one on the left...' he whispered, 'and I'll look after its mate,' he continued, and they both delved deep into their satchels to see what could be used as a weapon. 'I can only find a length of rope...' Fluke looked up in dismay, 'how's that going to help?' and watched to see what Tash could find in her satchel.

'Tie it into a loop and make a lasso,' she said and got busy with her paws, eventually satisfied with her efforts. 'We'll just have to tie them up for now.'

Fluke and Tash strode out into the open, swirling their ropes around their heads, which caused the startled soldier ants to turn around. They both let loose their homemade lassoes and watched. Tash's rope found its target and settled around the midriff of a surprised ant, but Fluke's ant was stirred into action and moved, causing him to miss his target and to snag his lasso over a large rock.

Tash pulled firmly on her rope causing the ant to drop its spear and struggle to get free. Fluke dropped his rope and dashed forward, picked up the loose spear and bopped it on the head of Tash's prisoner, he then turned his attention to the second ant.

They both stood staring at each other. Fluke leapt into action and used the spear as a sword. The ant, not used to any sort of action down here, dropped his weapon and turned to flee, tripped over Fluke's rope and fell into a heap on the floor next to his companion.

Fluke gently bopped him on the head as well and Tash tied the two ants together.

'They'll be OK Fluke,' she said, finishing off with a sturdy knot, 'they might have sore heads after you knocked them out but they'll sleep it off, and hopefully give us enough time to find the Nummers.'

Time to free the slaves...

Papa nudged Mama and smiled as they followed Dice and Nat down a long passage. One ant was leading the way with their friendly ant following behind. As far as anybody watching could tell, it looked just like a slave party being taken to work.

They entered into a small chamber and stopped, huddled together unsure what would happen next. One ant raised Mama's arms in front of her and with the use of his sharp spear he cut through her bindings and set her free. The second ant joined in and helped released Papa, Nat and Dice.

'Why are you letting us go?' asked Mama, glad to be free but slightly confused.

The friendly ant sighed and shook his head. 'We're not all bad down here you know, most of us are being forced to work like all of you...' he pointed around the small room. 'A few of us have had enough. It's not right enslaving us all and forcing us to work. We've decided to free as many as we can and get out before we get caught. We want a normal way of life, like it used to be, before these hairy, two legged creatures took over and made us work for them.'

'So what now?' Nat asked.

'You act as if you're still our prisoners. We'll go around with you and together we'll release as many of the dinosaurs as possible. You whisper to them, explain what's happening, and have them pretend to be tied up. When their work shift has finished, and everybody has settled down for the night, we're all to meet by the large rock pool.'

'Why the large rock pool?' asked Papa.

'There's a secret passage nearby which leads right up through the volcano to the surface and has a concealed entrance near the top. It's the only exit that we know of without having to go out the main entrance and alerting the guards.'

It was agreed that in four hours, when the guards were asleep or resting, the escape committee would meet and hopefully make a dash for freedom.

Over there...

Fluke followed Tash round yet another bend and came to a ledge with a set of steps leading down to a large open spaced cavern, where a huge building was currently under construction.

Teams of dinosaurs, under the watchful gaze of several of the *Bigfoot tribe*, were currently hoisting another large building block into place. Creeping forward to get a better look they both peeped over the edge and saw to their delight the Nummers with two dinosaurs. It seemed from their vantage point that all four were tethered together and had two soldier ants guarding them.

'Over there Tash...' whispered Fluke and pointed.

'Yep, I see them Fluke. Well at least we know they're both safe. Now all we have to do is follow them, get rid of their two guards and whisk them to safety,' said Tash, trying to work out a plan.

The Nummers and the two dinosaurs got close to the other workers and when *Bigfoot* was looking the other way something happened and hushed words were exchanged. The dinosaurs briefly nodded and carried on as if nothing had happened or been said, and from this distance it was hard for Fluke and Tash to see or hear what had happened.

The two soldier ants guarding the Nummers took them off around another bend and down a new tunnel. Fluke and Tash ducked down behind the rock and crept down the steps, pausing midway, not wishing to alert the *Bigfoot* to their presence.

Satisfied that the *Bigfoot* creatures were looking in the opposite direction, Fluke followed Tash and they hurried down the tunnel in hot pursuit of the Nummers.

'It's getting warmer Tash,' said Fluke, mopping his forehead with the back of his paw.

'Well, we are in a volcano Fluke and you are wearing a fur coat,' joked Tash, who was also feeling the increased temperature. 'We must be getting closer to the lava flow,' she said.

Minutes later they had caught up with the four prisoners and two soldier ants.

'Come on Fluke, all this sneaking round is getting tiresome,' whispered Tash, hiding around a bend in the tunnel, 'grab your spear and lets confront those two guards and then we can get out of here,' and they both leapt out to attack the two soldier ants.

Charging down the tunnel, spears pointed, they were ready for action and with all their recent training by Robin Hood and Addaya, from their Egyptian adventure, they felt that two soldier ants shouldn't be a problem to deal with.

Fluke was ready to pounce when he heard a female voice shout '*Nooooo Fluke,*' which confused Fluke and stopped him in his tracks.

Papa turned around to see what all the fuss was about and a huge smile spread over his face. 'You two took your time!' joked Papa, 'but are we glad to see you again.'

'What about the guards?' asked Tash, spear poised as she too was also ready to pounce on one of the two ants.

'They're friends Tash,' said Mama and rushed over to give Fluke and Tash a big welcome hug, 'they're helping us escape. We've been going around all the different groups of dinosaur slaves to release them and arrange a meeting point later tonight.'

Papa joined in the conversation, 'and in a short while we've all got to meet by the large rock pool. There's a tunnel which leads right up to the surface so we can all get out of here together.'

'Sorry about nearly attacking you,' said Fluke turning to one of the soldier ants, 'we weren't to know,' and they shook paws in a friendly greeting.

'That's OK,' the ant replied, 'but we have to be very careful from now on as our masters won't be too happy when they find out what's about to happen.'

'*Bigfoot* you mean?' whispered Tash looking all round, 'now that really was a surprise to see the *Sasquatch*, as they are also called.'

'I also call them big hairy apes,' laughed Fluke, but nervously looked all around just in case any of them were nearby.

'So you've seen them then?' asked Mama.

'Outside the main entrance,' confirmed Tash, 'and they do exist, well at least they look like the *Bigfoot* that's been sighted around the North American forests and aren't just a myth like the so called experts tell everyone,' said Tash.

The *Bigfoot* tribe...

With only one more small group of dinosaurs to be freed, hopefully they'd all soon be out of here and could make their way back home to their respective herds and get back to a normal dinosaur life.

Fluke and Tash joined in and went in search of the final group to confirm the time and place for them to meet up later.

Fluke was deep in thought and asked, 'just been thinking Nat, but is it wise to meet up together in one large group? Wouldn't it make more sense to have smaller escape parties, you know, less chance of being spotted?'

'I see what you mean Fluke, but there's only one escape tunnel that we can use as the main entrance is too well guarded, and just in case it all goes wrong we can at least help each other,' said Nat, hoping nothing would go wrong.

The excitement spreading through the rest of the volcano was infectious. Each group quietly talked to each other about the great escape happening tonight.

Unfortunately one small group got a bit too excited and without realising, revealed the plans. Two soldier ants, still loyal followers of the *Bigfoot tribe,* overheard and reported back. The *Bigfoots* weren't impressed and hastily arranged their own meeting to discuss plans to foil the escape.

The spacious cavern which housed the large rock pool, the one Fluke and Tash had used to enter the volcano, was slowly filling up with random dinosaurs. They milled around waiting for the rest to arrive, trying to be quiet, but the excitement was too much for some, the thought that they would soon be able to escape and get home to see friends and family was exciting. Some glanced into the rock pool wondering if they could swim to freedom, but then discounted the idea as they weren't very good swimmers.

'Why are we waiting?' asked a Lophorhothon pacing nervously up and down.

'You know why,' replied Styg impatiently, a Stygimoloch who stood on her hind feet looking around the room. 'We're waiting for the Nummers, Dice, Nat and the two friendly ants. They've got to show us the right escape tunnel. You take the wrong passage and you'll be stuck down here for ever,' she finished.

More dinosaurs filled the room. All heads turned to view the newcomers and words of greeting were shared, but still no sight or sound of the Nummers group.

They're surely not going to throw stones...

The escape committee led by Fluke, Tash, the Nummers and Nat, finally agreed that they'd managed to get the message to everybody.

'They should all be waiting at the meeting point, the rock pool, by now,' Papa said, 'we best head that way ourselves.'

'Yeah, you can't be late for your own escape!' joked Fluke and followed Nat as they walked off.

They entered the chamber with the lava flow, a river of red bubbling, very, very hot magma. The only way to reach the meeting point was through the tunnel at the far end, and as they made their way over, the two ants slowed and eventually halted.

'C'mon, why have we stopped?' asked Fluke, as he bumped into the back of Tash. He hadn't been watching where he was going as he'd been staring in awe at the river of bubbling red hot lava. Looking up to see what the problem was he gulped nervously, 'oops, *Bigfoot*, that's why,' he muttered.

There, blocking the exit were a line of the huge, hairy ape-like creatures and they didn't look very happy.

Fluke tapped Tash on the shoulder, 'do you think they might be a tiny bit annoyed that everybody is trying to escape?'

With a red hot lava flow behind them, and a line of angry *Bigfoot* in front, Tash couldn't help herself and laughed, 'yes Fluke,' she shook her head and tittered, 'they don't look too happy do they,' and watched as one-by-one the hairy apes each lifted massive boulders above their heads. The strength of these creatures was breathtaking, their muscles bulged under hairy skin and bright scary yellow eyes glared back in anger.

'They're not really going to throw those stones at us are they?' Tash asked and then ducked as the first huge boulder headed their way, thankfully sailing over her head and landing behind.

'Stones?' said Fluke, who then ducked, 'those are pretty large stones Tash!' he exclaimed, skilfully dodging another missile that had been hurled at them.

A steady rain of rocks, some medium size and some extremely large, flew through the air as each *Bigfoot* released its own stash of large boulders.

'Take cover everybody!' hollered Tash over the din caused by crashing boulders, thankfully nobody had yet been hit.

Fluke quickly looked over his shoulder at the carnage of boulders strewn over the volcano floor. 'Err Tash,' he said and gently tapped her shoulder.

'Not now Fluke, I'm a bit busy trying to avoid being hit,' she replied whilst side-stepping another projectile.

'Tash, I really think you should take a look,' he tapped her shoulder with more urgency, 'seriously, I think you should look behind us.'

'Why?' said Tash and turned to see what the fuss was all about. 'Now we're in trouble,' she muttered.

Building a dam...

Now the *Bigfoot Tribe* might be big, strong and be able to lift boulders the size of a small family car, but thankfully they were lousy shots and couldn't aim their throws very well. Because they had missed their intended targets, the boulders had overshot the mark and landed directly in the lava flow. Huge boulders were piling up, more being added each time one was hurled through the air.

'They've only gone and built a dam!' said Tash, shaking her head in disbelief.

'Yes, and now that the lava flow has been diverted from its natural course its burst its banks and is flooding the cavern floor,' said Fluke, staring in horror and fascination in equal measures as the red hot liquid began gathering pace and heading directly towards them.

Fluke and Tash stared in silence at each other for a couple of seconds that felt like minutes. Tash broke the silence first, 'OK, so we charge the *Bigfoot* and hope they get out of the way.'

'Charge the *Bigfoot*?' asked Fluke.

'It's either that or get our paws burned Fluke,' and she turned to face the hairy beasts, raised her spear and prepared.

Bigfoots' large hairy nostrils flared at the smell of the fiery red liquid and their evil yellow eyes widened in horror, as they too noticed the lava flow heading their way. They were surprised too when they heard a bone-chilling cry of "*chaaaaaarge!*" They scattered like a set of ten pins down a bowling alley, disappearing down different tunnels in their panic to flee the area of fiery magma.

Tash in front, closely followed by Fluke, Nat and Dice, with the two ants bringing up the rear, went down another tunnel, which they hoped would lead them back to the rock pool, when they ran into the dinosaurs waiting patiently for the escape committee.

Hasty introductions were made as the two ants pointed to a large boulder. 'That needs moving,' pointing to a large rock, 'it's blocking the entrance to the tunnel.'

The bigger dinosaurs, along with Fluke and Tash, stood around the boulder and put all their effort into trying to move it.

A lot of grunting and sore paws were all they got from their efforts, as the boulder didn't seem to want to move much. It rocked back and forth a few inches, occasionally revealing a gap and a teasing view of the escape tunnel before it fell back into place.

'If only we had a stick of dynamite, we'd move it no problem,' panted Fluke, rubbing his paws together in preparation for another struggle with the pesky rock blocking their path.

'Well, we'll have to push harder Fluke, as we don't have any sticks of dynamite,' said Tash.

Panicked voices could be heard coming from the back of the cavern and dinosaurs began pushing each other. Fearing the *Bigfoot* had returned again, Tash looked over her shoulder at the melee taking place and realised with horror it wasn't Bigfoot but the lava flow. It had built up speed and had followed them down the tunnel and was creeping into the cavern.

Tash looked at the lava. She moved her head and followed what she thought would be its natural course and smiled, 'maybe we won't need dynamite after all Fluke, as that lava is heading directly towards the water.'

'Water? How will water help?' asked a confused Fluke and watched as dinosaurs stood as far back as they could get, staring in fear as the flow of lava crept past.

Outside the volcano...

$\mathcal{A}$mos was pacing up and down. Fluke and Tash had been gone for what seemed like ages and he was now one very deeply worried dinosaur. He had been given some detailed instructions by Tash on things that they could do to help if and when they escaped the volcano.

The work that Tash had asked them to do had kept Amos, Tops and Peter busy for a while, but now they were stood waiting, and waiting was the worst.

'Do you think they're OK?' Amos asked for the tenth time.

'They'll be fine, I'm sure of it,' replied Tops and Peter together.

Tops walked off to check one of the traps they had set. It was a large pit in the ground they had dug and covered the hole with branches to hide it from view.

The trap was set around the corner from the main entrance to the volcano. If and when Fluke and Tash were chased out of the volcano they would all surely head this way and hopefully any chasing soldier ants and the hairy beasts, that

Tash had called *Bigfoot,* would fall in. Tops was anxious for their new friends as well and this was probably the fourth time he had checked the trap.

Peter wandered off to check on trap two. It was a backup plan in case anybody avoided trap one and consisted of a big pile of logs stacked up on the side of a hill, supported by one large stick with a vine tied around it. A trip wire was stretched across the path and if the wire was activated it would release the stick, causing the stacked logs to come tumbling down the side of the hill causing panic and confusion to any of the chasers.

A deep rumbling noise came from within the volcano and the ground began to shake which caused them all to stop what they were doing. They huddled together and looked towards the volcano fully expecting red hot lava to start gushing out the top. To say they were surprised at what came out the volcano rim was putting it mildly.

'Is that who I think it is…?' said Amos and turned to his colleagues for confirmation. They all looked at each other and burst out laughing.

The world's first water chute...

'*E*verybody take cover as best as you can, there's going to be an explosion!' shouted Tash and watched as dinosaurs fled to the furthest corners of the cavern.

'Thought you said we didn't have any dynamite?' asked Fluke.

'Hydro volcanism,' replied Tash, 'and it can be quite spectacular to watch.

'Hydro *what*?' said Fluke more confused than ever.

'"*Hydro*" as in water, and "*volcanism*", well, as in a volcano Fluke. It's when red hot magma from the volcano and water combine causing a steam explosion. It might be enough to shift that large boulder blocking our escape route.'

And it was more than enough, in fact way more than anybody could expect. The magma flow poured into the rock pool and instantly a huge geyser of steam shot into the air causing the ground and whole volcano to shake. An underwater explosion occurred. The large boulder was dislodged as easily as someone flicking a marble across the floor, but what happened next surprised even Tash.

The ground shaking had dislodged more rocks, and as they came tumbling down from the ceiling they stopped the magma flow from entering the cavern, completely sealing everybody inside.

'Now we're completely trapped Tash,' said Fluke, 'I just hope the escape tunnel leads all the way to the surface.'

A huge water fountain caused by the explosion shot up from the rock pool. It was as if all the water from the lake had been sucked up and funnelled directly into the cavern.

With nowhere for the water to go but upwards, Fluke, Tash, the Nummers and all the dinosaurs were lifted off their paws to the top of the water fountain and catapulted skywards. Higher and higher they went, the tunnel walls shot passed at some speed. Looking upwards, Tash spied the bright daylight getting brighter the closer they got to the volcano rim.

'It's like being at a huge water park,' shouted Fluke happily at the top of his voice, trying to be heard over the din that the fountain of water was making.

The volcano's water fountain ejected them from the inside and they shot into open air. Gravity eventually took over and they all landed in a torrent of gushing water part way down the slope of the volcano. Water continued to erupt from the top and was creating a massive water slide.

'Yeeha!' said Tash, who was certainly enjoying the water chute ride down to the base of the volcano. Eventually the water stopped flowing and dried up.

A scene of peace and calm followed. No more explosions were heard from within the volcano and as everybody realised they were now safe they picked themselves up, dusted themselves down, gathered around and walked the rest of the way down the steep sloping side of the volcano.

'Well, wasn't that fun,' said a joyful Fluke, a huge grin spread over his face.

Tash heartily agreed. 'Well, that's one way to leave a volcano,' and then proceeded to carry out a head count to make sure everybody was present.

A few dinosaurs had minor cuts and bruises but nothing too much to worry about, it was the least anybody could expect after being shot like a cannonball from the top of a volcano.

'Fluke, Tash, and oh my, it's Nat,' said an excited, but familiar voice. Turning around, Fluke and Tash saw Amos and the gang striding over to welcome them.

Nat trotted over to his old friends, and Amos, Tops and Nat all began speaking at once, such was the joy of their re-union.

As the greetings carried on, around the corner trundled a mixed herd of dinosaurs led by Amos's dad. The herd consisted of *Lophorhothons*, *Stygimolochs*, *Troodons*, a couple of *Triceratopses* and Nat's dad, an *Anatotitan,* plus others.

They might have arrived a bit late to get involved in the rescue but it was still a touching sight, as each of the young dinosaurs recently freed found one of their parents and a huge celebration was started.

Tash looked around and noted that Peter had wandered off to the side-lines, keeping himself away from the celebrations. Tapping Fluke on the shoulder and dragging him away from a conversation with Nat's dad, he pointed to a sad looking Peter. Fluke immediately understood and followed Tash.

Back to the hill...

Peter looked up as his two friends, Fluke and Tash, approached. He brightened and said happily, 'everything turned out well didn't it? The rescue mission was successful and it's great to see all the families back together again.'

'About that Peter. You know we've not forgotten our promise to you about finding your family, don't you?' said Tash nudging Fluke to say something and get involved.

'Thing is Peter, your family are up there somewhere...' Fluke pointed towards the sky, 'and you're still down here on the ground, so how about we get you up there flying? We'll get you over your fear of heights, won't we Tash?' Fluke said kindly.

It was agreed, they would go back to where their adventure had first started and start searching for Peter's family. Tash was certain his family would miss him and come back to look for their son.

The mixed dinosaur herds left the volcano far, far behind. They left together but eventually the large group began to split up, different dinosaurs heading in different directions. Each time someone left the group fond farewells and goodbyes were exchanged, with the promise they would surely see each other again on some open plain again someday.

The remaining group had dwindled in size until it was only Fluke, Tash, the Nummers, Peter, Amos, Tops, Nat and Nat's dad. Dice had said his fond farewells to everyone the day before, as he wanted to try his luck by heading north to see what was there, "and anything would be an adventure," he joked, "except for more volcanos."

Three long days of hiking lay ahead for the rest of the group as they had universally decided to take a long detour away from the swamp, none of them wanted to risk passing through there again.

Tired and weary, but glad to be back in familiar surroundings, quick hellos where exchanged with Amos, Nat and Tops' families. They had agreed to meet in two hours at the top of Amos's favourite hill overlooking the valley, which spread out below.

Flying lessons...

Fluke, Tash and the Nummers stood and waited patiently with Peter for Amos, Tops and Nat to arrive.

Once they were all safely gathered, Fluke said, 'wow Amos, I can see why you love it up here, the views are amazing,' and watched in awe as swooping Pteranodons filled the sky and herds of roaming dinosaurs walked across the valley floor. Dinosaur life appeared to be back to normal. It was a truly spectacular sight and would never be forgotten.

Tash coughed politely to get everyone's attention. 'OK, so now for the reason we've all gathered here, which of course is to help, encourage and watch our good friend Peter get over his fear of heights by giving him flying lessons.'

'Oh, I'm not sure,' said Peter nervously looking down from the great height of the hill, 'I feel jittery just stood up here, let alone flying high up there,' he said pointing to the circling reptiles.

'Look, Peter,' said Fluke, putting a comforting paw around Peter's shoulder, 'I hated water and I couldn't swim before I came here. If I can conquer my fear of water then you can beat your fear of heights,' he continued with loads of encouragement.

'And we'd never flown before, had we dearest?' said Mama turning to Papa, 'and if we managed to fly without wings, I'm sure you'll be just fine.'

Peter sighed, and then grinned, 'OK, it's a deal. What are we waiting for?' and began flapping his wings in readiness.

'Hold on Peter,' laughed Tash, 'we're going to give you a head start,' and dragged their magic case out. Peter watched as Fluke and Tash hopped aboard and beckoned Peter to follow.

Sitting comfortably Tash started the controls by turning the handle. The case hovered a few inches off the floor, whilst the rest all watched in fascination.

The case took to the air with Fluke whooping with glee. Tash looked around and laughed, 'you can open your eyes now Peter, it's perfectly safe,' and watched as Peter slowly opened them and stared at his surroundings.

How to make a dinosaur kite...

'Fluke, can you tie some rope around one of Peter's ankles and hang onto the other end as tight as you can?' Tash waited patiently for Fluke to carry out the task. Satisfied the rope was tied securely to Peter, she then encouraged Peter to stretch his wings to their full span.

Almost immediately Peter lifted off from the case and took to the air like a kite. With Fluke hanging onto one end of the rope, Peter started flying above their heads. He flapped his wings a bit which kept him a few feet above the case.

'How is it Peter?' asked Tash, glancing up.

'This is fantastic Tash, flying is easy, I can't understand why I was ever worried about it before!' and he banked to the left. Tash watched the course that Peter took and steered the case to follow.

'I can't believe we've made a real life dinosaur kite,' chuckled Fluke, hanging onto the rope with his paw. 'You're leading us now Peter, so whichever way you go we'll follow,' confirmed Fluke. Ten more minutes of high altitude flying followed, then Tash turned around and said 'OK Fluke, time to release the rope from Peter.'

The rope had been tied in such a way that with a gentle tug and a certain flick of the wrist, the knot tied around Peter's ankle came free, allowing Peter to fly all by himself. He glanced down and noticed he was on his own, a smile reached his face, he'd conquered his fear of flying, which made him so happy.

The case came to a soft landing on the hill and nestled beside the Nummers and Amos. Peter followed soon after and they were all stood together. The group congratulated Peter on his exploits and he could feel himself blush under the onslaught of praise heading his way. At that moment Peter heard a familiar voice from above.

'Well done son, we knew you could fly.' Peter looked up and saw to his delight his parents, brother and sisters circling overhead. Peter shed a tear, but it was a tear of happiness, as he knew it was time to say goodbye to all his new friends as he must re-join his family.

Fluke and Tash had a lump in their throats too as they bid farewell to their new friend and watched as Peter flapped and stretched his giant wings, and took to the air. The whole family of Pteranodons circled above, and just before they departed, Peter dipped his wings to the left and then to the right, as if waving goodbye.

It wasn't until they could no longer see the departing Pteranodons that Tash sighed and said, 'well, as great as it's been, and let me tell you it's been one of the best adventures ever, it's time we started to think about going home.'

Home time...

'We can't believe it's time for you all to go,' sniffed Amos, Tops and Nat, all three were so glad they'd made some great new friends, but were deeply sad that they all had to head off home.

'We'll be thinking of you, won't we?' said Fluke to his colleagues. Tash and the Nummers totally agreed.

'It's certainly been an experience,' laughed Papa, and leapt aboard the magic case and sat behind Mama, waiting for Fluke and Tash to join them.

Tash turned to Fluke, and with a lingering last look around, her eyes strayed to the far off distant volcano. Plumes of smoke were drifting lazily from its rim, the water fountain having long since been replaced with the more traditional smoke.

'So do you think that the *Bigfoots* have been sealed inside for ever and ever?' she asked.

'Probably,' confirmed Fluke, 'it was a massive explosion inside and with the ceiling collapsing all around, escape from that would have been very difficult.'

'We escaped Fluke,' said Tash deep in thought, 'and don't forget the *Bigfoot* and *Sasquatch* sightings that have been reported in our lifetime Fluke, maybe it's just possible that a small number of them did escape and were left to live their lives in secret and roam the forests.'

It was time to go. Tash sat at the front, the Nummers in the middle with Fluke sat snuggly at the back.

'Fluke and Tash airways welcomes its passengers on-board and we hope you enjoy the flight home,' laughed Fluke.

'We will Fluke, but please, please can we avoid any more rogue Pteranodons, I really don't think I could go through that again,' laughed Mama.

'No worries, we'll be home before you realise it,' said Tash, as she set the controls, turned the handle three times and then, as they were all waving goodbye, the case promptly vanished into thin air.

12:24...

The case materialised from thin air, skidded across the bedroom carpet and nestled snuggly up against the waiting wardrobe. The Nummers slowly opened their eyes and gazed around the bedroom, carefully stepping down off the case, they breathed a huge sigh of relief.

Fluke looked over at the digital clock on the bedside table, noticed the time said 12:24, and said, 'well done Captain Tash, home on time as usual,' and then helped Tash open the wardrobe doors and store their case back inside, tucked away at the rear, hidden behind a line of jackets and coats.

'Well, thank you both,' said Mama. Glancing at the clock she laughed, 'we left at 12:22 and returned at 12:24, how come we've managed to cram so much adventure into two minutes?' and then joined in with Papa as they started to yawn, the last few days of adventure and excitement had caught up with them.

They said their good nights and disappeared down the stairs, making their way out of the cat flap and across the lawn, heading back home to their tree stump.

Fluke was watching them cross the lawn when the security light switched on and flooded the garden with artificial light. He leant out of the window and whispered, 'mind the pair of Tyrannosaurus hiding behind the honeysuckle and apple trees,' and closed the window whilst chuckling to himself.

Victorian Adventure...

Fluke and Tash checked around and were happy the room was neat and tidy, just how they had found it. Tiptoeing across the landing they ducked underneath the ironing board and flopped on the sofa.

Stretching to help relieve their aching muscles they got comfortable and settled down for a well-earned night's sleep.

'What an adventure Tash,' yawned Fluke, scratching an itchy spot behind his ear, 'and some amazing friends we've made.'

'We'll miss them, that's for sure,' replied Tash, who stifled a yawn herself. 'I still can't believe we've met *Bigfoot,* been stranded inside a volcano, you were nearly eaten by a giant Venus Flytrap, I was nearly dinner for a swamp monster and we've both escaped the clutches of a pair of vicious Tyrannosaurus Rex,' she chuckled, 'and we've taken the Nummers away for a trip they won't forget.'

'I know we've only just got back Tash, but it's nice to plan ahead, so where do you fancy going for our next adventure?' asked Fluke looking at

Tash in the darkened room, the only light visible came through the blinds from the street lamp outside their bedroom window.

Tash noticed the street lamps and a thought struck her. 'Gas lamps!'

'Gas lamps?' asked Fluke.

'No electricity Fluke, they had to use gas lamps. How about Victorian London, Fluke?'

'Victorian London? Hmmm, sounds interesting,' said Fluke.

'So much happened back then Fluke. You had Charles Dickens writing his classics, Arthur Conan Doyle with his Sherlock Holmes books, Florence Nightingale was travelling the world nursing, Alexander Graham Bell invented the telephone, Charles Darwin was around and the famous clock *Big Ben* outside the Houses of Parliament was just finished.'

The era was decided, it just remained to be seen on the exact date they would choose. The pair of time travellers drifted off to sleep dreaming of their new adventure.

ISBN: 978-0-9934956-0-1

ISBN: 978-0-9934956-3-2

ISBN: 978-0-9934956-6-3